Emerson put her strong, agile fingers inside. Hope closed her eyes and gripped the pillow behind her. They both waited for the oncoming quiver. Hope let go with the abandon of having wanted this for weeks, of needing to feel alive and filled with desire. They barely got Emerson's clothes off before Hope pulled Emerson on top and gently made her cry out with the sheer pleasure of being in love and being touched again.

About the Author

Saxon Bennett lives in Phoenix, Arizona, for purposes of sun worship and Technicolor dreaming. Phoenix is a place full of human oddities and transcendental tree huggers. And, like the middle of an Oreo cookie, she feels perfectly at home.

A Question of Love

BY
SAXON BENNETT

THE NAIAD PRESS, INC.
1998

Printed in the United States of America on acid-free paper
First Edition

Editor: Lila Empson
Cover designer: Bonnie Liss (Phoenix Graphics)
Typesetter: Sandi Stancil

Library of Congress Cataloging-in-Publication Data

Bennett, Saxon, 1961 –
    A question of love / by Saxon Bennett
        p.   cm.
    ISBN 1-56280-205-4 (pbk.)
    1. Lesbians – Fiction   I.Title.
PS3552.E547544Q47   1998
813'.54—dc21   97-40428
                                                            CIP

To Lin,
for being my wondrous accident.
What would we have done without
the playful hand of providence?

And to Crappapore,
for whiskers in the morning, tuna breath,
and all those howling expletives every Sunday.

One

There was a scuffle up the street, and two old ladies screeched in near unison. Rachel grabbed Hope's arm and pulled her into the doorway of the greengrocer's. A streak of human flesh raced by on a pair of rollerblades, jumped over the fire hydrant, sidestepped the produce stand, and yelled "Hey!" before coming to an abrupt stop and whirling around to greet Rachel.

A young woman in a torn T-shirt, cutoffs showing the boxers beneath, and a baseball hat turned backward stood grinning at Rachel.

"Glad to see you're still a perfect heathen," Rachel said.

"You don't approve of my tomboy image?"

"No, it's your skating that petrifies me. You make the bladers in New York seem tame. Have you got any more citations to add to your collection?"

"Yeah, Sheriff Bedford got me last week. Came around a corner too fast and nearly leveled a tour bus full of elderly shoppers as they were exiting the vehicle. I didn't hit anybody, but I mucked Mayor Lasbeer's Mercedes-Benz when I was forced to take a detour across the hood. I took a little paint with me."

Hope Kaznot burst out laughing. Both Rachel and Emerson turned to look at her.

"I don't mean to laugh. I hope you weren't hurt," Hope said, wiping her eyes with the corner of her shirt.

"You'll have to forgive her; she hasn't laughed in weeks. I think you broke the spell," Rachel explained.

Emerson cocked her head and eyed Hope across the top of her dark sunglasses. "So who's your pretty little friend?" she inquired.

"Hope Kaznot, meet Emerson Wells," Rachel said.

Hope tentatively stuck out her little hand, and Emerson gently shook it.

"Hope is staying the summer with me," Rachel said.

"Girlfriend?" Emerson asked.

"No, she's running away from her girlfriend," Rachel explained.

"Rachel!" Hope said.

"Well, are you?' Emerson asked.

Hope wasn't entirely certain she was cut out for small-town life. In Heroy nothing was sacred, decorum was thrown to the seven winds, and honesty was the flavor of the month at the existential ice-cream stand. Hope found it alarming. She was a product of a well-bred Boston family where one didn't discuss the little tremors that flowed beneath everyone's polished exterior.

Leaving her girlfriend because she was suffering from an acute case of nervous tension, a polite term for a nervous breakdown, was not something she wished to discuss with a perfect stranger. Anyone who had spent the last three years with Pamela Severson was bound to suffer from a few things.

Hope unwillingly confessed, "Yes, I'm taking a break from my overly-ambitious, highly-talented dynamo of a girlfriend."

"And that's all right with her?" Emerson inquired.

"Well, she's not ecstatic about it."

"Everyone needs to take a breather now and then," Rachel said.

"You're staying the summer?" Emerson asked, obviously contemplating the possibilities of having someone new in town.

"Yes she is, and I expect you to help entertain her. In a suitable fashion, of course," Rachel added, suddenly aware once again of Emerson's less-than-orthodox behavior.

"Hmm," Emerson said, skating off and then turning back around. "We'll see about that."

Hope and Rachel arrived at the café that Rachel's mother, Katherine, owned and operated. Rachel would be working there this summer. Hope was to rest. She

3

was embarrassed by her inability to handle her life, but she knew she needed to relax, gain weight, and sleep.

Hope would have spent the summer in New York, dealing with Pamela and calling Rachel in tears every afternoon had an intense young doctor not been adamant about getting her somewhere quiet — at a private hospital or out of town. Rachel had come up with the perfect plan. Right up until shutting the car door and waving good-bye, Pamela had stormed about using expansive hand movements to express her dislike as she harassed Hope for not being strong, for losing weight, for losing her mind. Hope had cowered and put off making definite plans for departure such as time, day, or century.

Until Rachel cornered her. It was late afternoon, and Pamela was away at one of her many faculty meetings. Hope was drinking a scotch and watching the light from the large bay window dance across the shiny wood floor of the loft. Rachel was pacing in long, even strides. Hope sat in her father's old leather chair, thoughtfully squeezing the arms, thinking about how both Pamela and her mother hated this chair. She'd rescued it from both of them, first when her father died and her mother closed up the Boston house and moved to Florida where she said it would clash with the decor and then from Pamela when they set up house together.

"That woman will be the death of you," Rachel said, referring to Pamela. "What I don't understand is why this is such a big deal. It's only for the summer. She won't even notice you're gone except maybe when she needs to make an appearance with her attractive girlfriend. The rest of the time she'll be off doing all those academic things she does. You spend more time with me than you do with her. We make a better couple, and we're not even lovers!" Rachel said, pouring Hope another scotch.

"Maybe we should be." Hope smiled.

Rachel melted. Hope was hard to resist with her tousled blond hair and blue eyes, sitting congenially in her favorite chair being screamed at by yet another overbearing woman. Rachel fell prostrate.

"I'm sorry. I'll take care of everything. You'll have time and space to breathe again. I promised my mom I'd help her with the café. There's a slew of art fairs coming through, and it's the height of tourist season. I'll go to work and you can hang out, sleep in, read, study some obscure Eastern philosophy . . . anything."

"I don't sleep, remember?" Hope said, trying to recall the last time she went to bed and found herself there in the morning. She usually ended up at Rachel's drinking scotch and watching old movies in the middle of the night. Maybe she should get her master's in film instead of women's studies.

Rachel went to school during the day and waited tables at night. She lived two doors down, and most nights Hope ended up there. Pamela, sleeping blissfully in the knowledge that she was well loved and successful, had no idea that her girlfriend was down the hall getting soused with another woman.

She got up each morning to find Hope sipping coffee and reading the paper. Pamela was taken by complete surprise when the doctors diagnosed Hope with a severe case of nervous tension. She was underweight, slightly malnourished, and sleep deprived. It wasn't until she fainted in class during an exam and the paramedics hauled her off that anyone realized she was sick.

"You need to rest. If you stay in the city she'll drag you around and make you nervous, and you'll never finish grad school because you'll be in the loony bin. Tell her that," Rachel said.

"Like she'd believe me," Hope replied. "She already thinks I'm an idiot."

"I hardly think so. You're her little protégé."

"No. I look good in a dinner jacket, and I know which fork to use."

"And you're good in bed," Rachel said, tousling her hair.

"How do you know that?" Hope asked indignantly.

"Pamela told me."

"She told you that!"

"It's nothing to be ashamed of. She was simply listing the proper attributes for the spouse of a rising lesbian academic star."

"They need to look good in a dinner jacket and fuck well," Hope said, getting up suddenly and pouring herself another scotch, wondering for half a second if she might have a drinking problem to add to her list of ailments.

"Why are you so angry?" Rachel asked, alarmed.

"Because I don't think I was put on this earth to be an attractive fuckmate for an aspiring academic whose life will not be complete until she has outshone every other lesbian feminist critic from the beginning of time and stretched across this pit hole we're calling a world. That does it. I'm going, and I don't give a shit what she says. Can I take my chair? I don't dare leave it with her," Hope asked, squeezing the top fondly.

"Sure. We'll strap it to the top of the car," Rachel replied.

Pamela was not happy when Hope told her she was going.

"I just don't understand it. You really should take better care of yourself, and you certainly can't expect me to wander around being a nurse, making sure you perform all the normal tasks the rest of us seem to manage. It's simple. You eat, you sleep, and you don't get sick. This is so typical of you to let things get out of hand. And now when I need you most you're set to run off. I don't want a psychotic partner. I don't have time for one."

"Then maybe you ought to find yourself a new one. You could place an ad — academic lesbian desires stunning, subdued wife who looks good in a dinner jacket, is well versed with the dry cleaners, and fucks well. That seems to be what you want. As far as I'm concerned, you can take your set of appropriate con-jugal attributes and shove it up your ass!"

Pamela slapped her.

With a welt still neatly imprinted on her cheek, Hope ran to Rachel's in tears. Rachel was furious.

"Just because you stood up for yourself for once

doesn't give her the right to hit you," Rachel said as she held a sobbing Hope in her arms. Hope spent the night.

The next afternoon when Hope got home, Pamela was waiting for her with flowers, apologies, and cowed eyes.

"I'm so sorry. I didn't mean to hurt you," Pamela said, tears welling up in her eyes. "I love you, dammit, and I'll miss you. But I want you to get better. If you need to get away for a while, I'll understand. I don't want to lose you."

"You won't; I promise."

Pamela carried her off to bed and gently made love to her, kissing her over and over again and trying to make the hurt they both were feeling go away.

"I'll never hit you again, I swear. Never, never."

"Shh, I know," Hope said. She fell asleep, her head on Pamela's shoulder, leaving her lover to gaze upon her and wonder why she had hurt her.

It was hard leaving. Pamela once again became the attentive, sensitive woman Hope had fallen in love with. But Hope couldn't help feeling a giant weight lifted from her chest. She could breathe again. As they hit the turnpike singing old Guess Who songs and smoking short cigars, she smiled.

"I love road trips," Rachel said, smiling and putting her sunglasses on as the sun started rise.

"Me too," Hope said, easing the seat back and squeezing Rachel's hand.

* * * * *

And now they were here sitting in Rachel's mother's café having Cokes and french fries and listening to old stories.

"If my mother's cooking doesn't make you fat, nothing will," Rachel said, slapping her thighs and dumping the rest of her fries on Hope's plate.

"You're perfect just the way you are," Hope said.

"I'm not fashionably lean."

"You don't have to be fashionably lean to be attractive."

"Do you find me attractive?" Rachel teased.

"Enormously so," Hope replied, putting her arm around Rachel's shoulders and kissing her cheek slightly.

"So, Hope, what do you think of our little town so far?" Katherine asked, surveying them and wondering where the boundaries lay.

Katherine Porter was a woman in her late fifties with short, gray hair. She wore faded men's work shirts, jeans, and boots, but she never looked completely butch. There was something undeniably feminine about her. She looked like a rancher's wife. She had large, brown eyes, and Hope had the uncanny sensation that she might fall into them one day never to be retrieved. It was nice to look at women with soft, earth-colored eyes. Rachel had her mother's eyes, and Hope had always longed for them at the end of a day spent with Pamela's fierce, steel-gray ones.

"The first person she met today was Emerson Wells, who nearly flattened us," Rachel said.

9

"Emerson . . ." Katherine said, smiling.

"My mother loves Emerson, more than me, sometimes," Rachel said good-naturedly.

"That's because you have a mother and she doesn't."

"What do you mean? The whole damn town treats her like family," Rachel said.

"This town wouldn't be here if it wasn't for the Emersons. Emerson's great-grandfather came out here and discovered copper. This was a mining town, then ghost town . . ."

"Then a mecca for gay and lesbian artists," Rachel piped in.

"It didn't start out that way."

"But it's that way now," Rachel said.

"So the whole town is gay?" Hope asked.

"Not the whole town, just most of the town," Rachel said.

"And everyone is okay with that?" Hope asked.

"Mostly, except for the two men who lost their wives to lesbians, but they've moved. The boys tried to put up a stink, you know, get the newspapers in Cedar City and Grover's Corner going, but all that did was increase the town's population. Shit, we've got artists from all over now, and it got us another art fair. The straight people in this town have been surrounded by it for so long I think they forgot what it's supposed be like," Katherine said, smiling at Hope.

"Damn, we've even got second-generation lesbians in this town; Rachel's one of them," Berlin said, coming around the corner carrying a tray of beers to the young women working on the tent crew for the art fair.

"Do you suppose I could have a scotch on the rocks?" Hope asked, eyeing the trayful of alcoholic beverages.

"Hallelujah, we've got another drinker in the house. Good for you, honey. A little liquor is not a bad thing. Just ask Berlin. She should be pickled by now, and look at her. Damn well preserved for her age. Not like this twelve-stepping lightweight over here," Katherine said, giving Rachel a tap on the top of her head.

"I am not a twelve-stepper. I drink. I just don't fall into ponds, down flights of stairs, and into the oleanders before I reach the front door," Rachel retorted.

Katherine shrugged her shoulders. "A couple of times we've got a little out of hand, but hell, that never hurt anyone," she said.

"Except the time Berlin got caught dressing up Dwight Emerson as the queen of England," Rachel said.

"Slight indiscretion. Besides, it was the Fourth of July, and Berlin is of English origin," Katherine said.

"If she's so English, how on earth did she end up with a name like Berlin O. Queen?" Rachel inquired.

"Honey, I told you. Berlin's mother was a cabaret singer during the war, the great one, and when she was forced out she went back to the mother country bitter. She died a bitter woman. I don't think there was a woman more pissed about that damn war than Berlin's mother. Ruined her career. Nothing worse than a ruined career to turn a woman's attitude, to turn her love worse. She named Berlin for her thwarted dreams," Katherine said, smiling over at Berlin, who was making small talk with the group of tent dykes in the corner.

Berlin was good for this town; she was the most personable one in it, and those women would be out barhopping by the time Berlin was done with them. Then they'd be in the café for a late-night bite or breakfast. Berlin O. Queen was the chamber of commerce.

Hope looked over at Berlin. She had scared the shit out of Hope that morning. It was awful. Hope was taking a bath. It was early. No one was up, so Hope thought she'd take a bubble bath and read. The lock on the bathroom door didn't work, but it seemed everyone was asleep. Next thing she knew this woman with green shit all over her face came screaming into the bathroom, turned on the water, and stepped in the tub before she noticed anyone was in it. Hope was mortified.

Berlin hit the water and turned to find someone else in the tub. She laughed hysterically while Hope tried desperately not to look at this older woman standing naked with one foot in the tub. Berlin swore they'd be friends forever since they met naked. Hope didn't quite comprehend her logic. Then Berlin asked if Hope would mind sharing the tub, and the two of them took a bath together. It wasn't as bad as she would have thought. They had a good talk. Hope told her about Pamela and the reason that she was here. Berlin seemed to understand.

12

At breakfast Hope kept thinking about how guests were treated in her family home, sequestered off somewhere, carefully tended and guarded against all forms of unpleasantness. It was strained at best. But in Rachel's family Hope was pulled tightly to their bosom and strapped there for the ride. Hope was beginning to think she preferred this.

Berlin sauntered back over. She was a pretty woman with voluptuous hips, breathing old-fashioned sensuality. Her tart British tongue had been softened with life in a small town, so it had an easy, rolling flavor to it, an odd mixture of intellectual redneckness.

"Say, darlings, I was thinking it's time for a dinner party, crystal and all, and some of my world-famous gumbo," Berlin said, tousling Hope's hair.

Rachel looked over at her queerly, recognizing in Berlin's gesture her own. She must have done that a thousand times.

"People do that to you a lot don't they?" Rachel said.

Hope smiled at her, thinking not everyone, not Pamela, or her mother, people who professed love but didn't show it.

"Why, darling, she just has tousling hair, fine, blond, and pretty and blue eyes to die for," Berlin said, as Hope looked up at her. "You're lucky I'm old and married, or honey I'd be courting you something fierce."

Hope blushed. Rachel smiled at her sympathetically and tousled her hair affectionately.

"Now about that dinner party. I thought we'd celebrate your arrival. Rachel, I'm leaving it up to you to trot over and talk Emerson into coming. She's been secluding herself again. Christ, here we are on the verge of the twenty-first century, and the woman refuses to have a telephone. And, honey, you need to get in touch with Lutz too," Berlin said, looking over at Katherine.

"I don't think it's a good idea to invite Mayor Lasbeer if Emerson is coming," Rachel said.

"But Lutz is such a character, and I'd hate for Hope to miss the chance of spending an evening with the town's most prominent member. Emerson and Lutz get along fine most of the time, excepting Emerson's traffic violations," Berlin said.

"Remember the Mercedes incident last week," Katherine reminded her.

"Hell, Emerson more than paid for the damages. Lord knows she's got enough money. Why she insists on living in that horrid brick building on Third Street is beyond me," Berlin said, shaking her head.

"It's a studio, Berlin," Rachel said.

"I don't care what you call it, the place is a pit, a pit to work in, maybe, but not to live in," Berlin said, emphatically.

"Emerson is an artist?" Hope inquired, trying to imagine the boyish young woman she met earlier as an artist.

"Sculptor, to be exact," Katherine replied, "a very talented one."

"Anyway, Rachel, you hop your butt over there while I take Hope shopping," Berlin said, taking off her apron.

Hope looked slightly alarmed.

"Don't worry, honey, I won't hurt you. After all,

we've bathed together," Berlin said, winking at her. "We've got things to talk about."

Rachel smiled at her. "I think you've been adopted."

Two

"So where's your pretty little friend?" Emerson asked, looking up from her work.

"Berlin dragged her off shopping. They've bonded ever since they shared a tub this morning," Rachel said, smiling.

"There's an image," Emerson said, getting up and wiping off her hands.

"What's this one called?" Rachel asked, fingering the model.

"Desire Leaves an Ugly Stain," Emerson said,

laughing. "I don't know. I just make the fuckers; my agent comes up with the groovy titles.

"God, I forget how beautiful these are, and big. It's weird to see yourself in metal, full-size, face-to-face."

"That's their power and appeal, my lovely. Speaking of that, are you posing for me this summer?" Emerson said, coming up to Rachel and taking a lock of her hair. Their eyes met. Emerson drew her near. "I've missed you," she whispered.

"You say that every year," Rachel said.

"You know these summertime romances," Emerson said, holding her, feeling their bodies melding again. Rachel was the only woman with whom she allowed herself these indulgences. Rachel pulled away gently.

She walked to the window and watched the street below, bustling with the tent crews and bitchy temperamental artists setting up their wares. The four California dykes were constructing yet another tent. Two blonds, a redhead, and a brunet — a type for any woman.

Rachel turned back around to find Emerson pulling clay from her nails with a palette knife.

"Emerson, how come you never found yourself another girlfriend?"

"After you broke my heart, women never seemed the same," Emerson replied, finishing up her pinkie nail.

Rachel pulled a Coke from the fridge. Emerson, like herself, was not much of a drinker. She had been once. She'd had a verifiable problem after Angel left. Sometimes Rachel wondered if their lives would have been different if Angel hadn't walked into them.

17

Would they have stayed lovers? It seemed that first lovers rarely make it. But they had been good first lovers, discovering each other's lovely intricacies with a relish held for the young. Rachel seldom felt that kind of lust anymore. And there had been lust, days when they couldn't get enough of each other; everything they did, everywhere they went was just another excuse to fuck. It was wonderful.

But then grown-up days set in. Rachel went to the East coast for college, and Emerson went to Paris to study. For a while they exchanged wonderful letters, and they spent one more summer together. And then everything changed.

Letters got fewer. There was the occasional indiscretion, the repentance. And then there was Angel. The summer Emerson didn't come home, there was no real word as to what was happening. Rachel was left to imagine. Her worst fear came true. Emerson came home with a new girlfriend, a wife, a grown-up lover, a beautiful woman named Angel. Emerson pleaded with Rachel to understand.

For two years both their lives were an awful mess. Rachel stayed away until she got an urgent call from her mother. Emerson was out of control. Angel had gone off to join the convent, something about not being able to fuse her love of Emerson with her overwhelming religious principles.

There was more destructiveness than Rachel had ever seen in Emerson, and then silence, quiet living, and the creation of the most beautiful pieces of sculpture wrought out from self-anguish, self-hatred, and burning love that no rain could quench. And now Rachel and Emerson were friends.

"Don't lie. It doesn't suit you. Angel cured you."

"And now I suppose you're going to say that like fine wine it's time someone opened the bottle," Emerson said, looking at her quizzically with those intense blue eyes.

Rachel smiled. "You know, sometimes I wished we could have met later, been each other's second or third lover. I would have liked to have been your wife."

"You would have made a good wife," Emerson said, taking her hand, standing next to her. "But we don't get a second chance, do we? Too much between us now. And speaking of girlfriends, where's yours?"

"Out there somewhere," Rachel said, sighing.

"You should try yourself on that pretty little friend of yours," Emerson said, taking a sip of Rachel's soda.

"Hope?"

"Yes, she seems nice. She looks a little fragile, but you always were good at taking care of us breakable ones."

"Not possible. Hope's girlfriend Pamela has an iron grip on her."

"A lot can happen in a summer, don't we know."

"Yes, now come for supper, eh, sixish. Speaking of Hope, I was kind of counting on you to help me do a little mending. She needs a friend, someone other than me to put a bit of joie de vivre back in her step. I think you two might like each other. She's not working this summer, and I don't want her moping about the house. I want her entertained, and you, it seems, have been guilty of hiding again. It will be good for both of you."

"I've been working," Emerson said, her arms outstretched and pointed to show a good many pieces.

19

"Too much and hiding. I know you, Emerson. You skate and you sculpt and you do both to get out of your body and your mind. You need to expand your horizons."

"And you think baby-sitting your pretty little friend is going to cure me of my demons?"

"Worth a try," Rachel said, heading for the door. "Six, remember? And you did make amends with Lutz, didn't you?"

"Of course. You'd think I was going to steal off in the night and leave town forever without paying. Yes, I paid all damages. She'll be there, I take it."

"Yes."

Three

"She's not coming," Katherine said, looking at her watch and fretting. It was half past six. "She's either on time or she's not coming. Rachel, she's got really bad. She can hardly drag herself out of that studio, and when she does she simply torments the town on those god-awful skates. She never stops to talk; she just scares the living daylights out of you when she goes whizzing by."

Berlin looked up from folding napkins. "Send Hope to fetch her," she said.

Everyone stopped and stared.

"Why Hope?" Rachel asked.

"Yes, why Hope?" Hope said, knowing somehow that Berlin was going to make her do yet another horridly extroverted thing, the third or so today.

"Because she's pretty," Berlin said.

Hope blushed.

"Emerson may be many things, but she is a Southern gentleman at heart. She can never turn down a pretty woman's request," Berlin stated emphatically.

Katherine's face lit up. "She's right. Hope, get going."

"But I don't even know where she lives," Hope said as Rachel pushed her to the door, "I don't even know her. You can't send a perfect stranger to fetch someone."

"In Heroy no one is a stranger. Right by the market, on the third floor, brick building. You can't miss it," Katherine said. "And tell her to hurry. It's almost ready."

Walking down the street, Hope jammed her hands in her pockets. I can't believe this is happening, she thought. I've bathed with a woman I just met who's old enough to be my mother. I'm to fetch someone I don't know who obviously doesn't want to come, and this is supposed to be restful. Hope scanned the horizon for the infamous brick building.

Up three horrific flights of stairs, the place looked like it should be condemned. She knocked at the door.

"I'm not coming!" a voice yelled from behind. "And you can't make me. I'm not feeling social, and I'm an adult in charge of my own life."

"Emerson, it's Hope. Please don't make me go

back empty-handed. It's awful enough being sent," Hope pleaded.

Scowling, Emerson opened the door to see if it was true. They had sent Hope, the miserable fuckers.

"Why'd they send you?"

"It's a long story."

"Well, I won't even consider your request unless you tell me what their tactics are."

"May I sit down?" Hope asked, feeling suddenly drained from the day.

Emerson let her pass. Hope did look rather pale.

"Would you like something to drink?"

"I don't suppose you have a scotch, do you?"

"No, but I can get you one."

"No, that's all right," Hope said, sighing.

"I'll be right back," Emerson said, flying out of the room before Hope had time to stop her. She flew to the bar on the corner.

"Jack, I need a scotch," Emerson told the grizzled old man behind the bar.

"I thought you gave all that up, Emerson," he said.

"I did. It's not for me; it's for the woman in my room. Maybe you should give me the bottle, and ice and a glass. I don't think I have a clean one."

"Plan on liquoring her up and then boinking her?" Dickie Sharpe asked, setting his beer down and fingering his pocket for a cigarette.

"Shut up, you stupid pervert!" Emerson said, laying money on the counter and whirling out of the bar.

"Yep, Dick, you sure got a way with the ladies,"
Jack said, laughing.

Hope heard Emerson flying up the steps two a
time, the bag of ice chinking alongside her.

"Emerson, I didn't need a drink that badly," Hope
said.

Emerson threw the ice in the sink and poured a
drink. "It's all right. The store is just on the corner."

"Everything in this town is just on the corner,"
Hope said, taking the drink. She eased back in her
chair.

"See, you look better already," Emerson said with
evident satisfaction.

"You really are a Southern gentleman, among
other things I'm sure."

"What do you mean?"

"That's what they said, that you were a Southern
gentleman at heart."

"And that's why they sent you?"

"Yes. They said you couldn't refuse a pretty
woman's request."

"They counted on you to do their dirty work."

"Yes," Hope said, blushing, her pale blue eyes
meeting Emerson's darker ones.

"Well, they were right. I can't," Emerson said.
This time she blushed.

"You'll come?" Hope said, sitting up.

"I have to clean up, and I haven't anything to
wear."

"I'll find you something. I like to pick out
clothes."

"What, are you going to run to the corner and buy me an outfit?" Emerson chided.

"No. I'm going to run you a bath and search your closet for something suitable," Hope said.

"And may I pour you another scotch? You seem to get remarkably extroverted after having just one," Emerson said, smiling.

"It's only because you're such a Southern gentleman and I feel like a belle."

"Perhaps, then, we should waltz," Emerson said, feeling inspired, taking Hope's hand and whisking her about the room before she had time to be shocked or blush. This was the queerest place, Hope thought.

"You dance beautifully, my dear," Emerson said.

"As do you, but I think your bath is about to overflow," Hope said, coming to a stop.

Emerson looked at the tubful of suds sitting out in the open. Living alone made one forget things like that.

Hope caught her gaze. "I won't look, I promise. You will, after all, be the second person I've shared the bathroom with today."

Hope sat down and covered her eyes while Emerson disrobed. Hope heard Emerson's body sink into the tub and said, "All clear?"

"Yes," Emerson said, smiling at her from beneath a mass of white bubbles.

"Where's your closet?" Hope said, pouring herself another scotch.

"In the bedroom," Emerson laughed.

"Why does it sound like you don't have one?" Hope said. "Do you have something against walls? I mean, you've got the whole third floor. Didn't it come with walls?"

"I had them all knocked out. I wanted one big room."

"Any particular reason?"

"I was feeling claustrophobic," Emerson ventured.

"Why don't I believe you?" Hope said, her head stuffed in an antique armoire.

"It's a long story. I'll have to tell you someday during the course of our blossoming friendship. Rachel says we should become friends, that we'd do each other good," Emerson told her.

"She does now, does she?" Hope said, laying out a soft gray sweater and a pair of black jeans on the bed, studying the effect.

"And why is that, do you suppose?" Emerson asked her.

"She thinks we're both nut cases," Hope said.

"Good guess."

"Well, maybe we should indulge her. Now stop dawdling," Hope said, pushing Emerson's head down in the water. She sat down on a stool, poured shampoo in her hand, and began washing Emerson's hair.

"You're really going to make me go, aren't you?" Emerson said.

"Yes, and in fact we're going to be grossly late."

"Do you always wash new acquaintances' hair?" Emerson asked suddenly.

"I thought we were friends?"

"Well, yes we are . . ." Emerson faltered.

"It's my one indulgence, my one successful attempt at throwing off a stuffy upbringing. I used to wash Pamela's hair all the time before she got too busy and started showering."

"Pamela, the girlfriend you ran away from?" Emerson asked.

"Yes," Hope said, massaging Emerson's neck. Emerson arched like a cat.

"Are you going back?"

Hope sighed. "I suppose I'll have to."

"Why?"

Hope pushed on her head. "Rinse," she commanded. "I don't know why."

"Maybe you'll find a reason not to go back," Emerson said.

"Yes, maybe," Hope said, handing her a towel and going to pour herself a third scotch.

"Well, how do I look?" Emerson said, after she'd dressed.

Hope came over and straightened the rolled neck of Emerson's sweater and then surveyed her, tucking a stray ringlet behind Emerson's ear. "Very good."

Four

"Are they going to be angry?" Hope asked as they trotted at a brisk pace up the hill to the house.

"No. They usually wrap up a plate and recount dinner stories while you gobble it down," Emerson said.

In fact, they wrapped up dinner and snacked on the hors d'oeuvre tray until there was nothing left but bones. They were engaged in a heated poker game when Hope and Emerson arrived.

Lutz was a poker fanatic of the worse kind. Lutz

was everything that frightened Hope rolled up into one person. She was loud, opinionated, aggressive, and large. Hope edged back toward the wall. Emerson took her hand.

"C'mon, we'll sneak back to the kitchen and find Katherine. She doesn't play poker. You can meet Lutz later. There'll be no talking to them until the game's over anyway," Emerson whispered.

It was true. No one appeared to notice they'd arrived. They heard only some heated discussion on poker rules or something.

Katherine was busy in the kitchen. Her face lit up when Emerson walked in the room.

"You two might as well eat. There'll be no stopping that business out there. They'll be eating at the poker table."

"I'm sorry, Katherine. I didn't mean to spoil your dinner party," Emerson said.

"Naw, honey, you didn't spoil it. I'm just glad you came. Good job, Hope. You two go sit in the dining room. No reason for the two of you not to have a nice dinner. I'll be right in."

The dining room shone with elegance, the silver and crystal on the lace tablecloth glimmering beneath candlelight.

"It's beautiful," Hope said.

"Katherine and Berlin know how to put on a classy dinner," Emerson agreed.

"I feel awful. We spoiled it," Hope said, sitting down looking rather crumpled.

"No, I spoiled it. But they'll have others, and a good poker game outshines anything else in this town. Wait, you'll see."

Katherine brought out rolls and two bowls of steaming gumbo. "The rest of the stuff is on the table, gals. Help yourself."

"Sit down, Katherine," Emerson said, taking her hand.

"Naw, honey, I've been snacking all night. 'Sides, I've got to keep things in line out there and keep feeding that endless pit they've got going," Katherine said, pulling Emerson to her and stroking her hair. "You've got to promise me things, darling," she said, looking down at her.

"I know," Emerson replied.

"Now, eat up. Emerson, open the wine for Hope."

Hope wondered what that meant but figured it would come with all the other things she would learn this summer.

After Emerson poured her a third glass of wine and herself another sparkling water, Hope asked, "You don't drink, do you?"

"Not anymore. It became a bit of a problem. More than a problem, really, but . . ." Her eyes met Hope's.

"Another long story?"

"Yeah," Emerson said, nodding her head, looking at the candlelight as it shimmered through her glass of water, and remembering.

Emerson hadn't drunk since Rachel fished her out of the pond that night. She'd almost drowned, yelling at Rachel to leave her alone, tears streaming down her face. She was covered in mud, wet to the core, and freezing cold. She told Rachel that she wanted to die there, drunk and puking in pond muck.

Rachel hauled her ass out of there and put her to bed, for days it seemed. Emerson had never been so sick in her whole life, a culmination of drunken screaming fits. Being jailed twice for disrupting convent life, standing on the hillside above the convent pleading to talk to Angel, the nuns finally being forced to have her dragged off, Angel refusing to see her.

"Will you tell me those stories someday?" Hope asked, their eyes meeting, measuring each other, promising things that didn't have names yet. A pregnant glance, full of unknown meaning.

That was how Berlin found them when she burst into the room. They both looked away quickly.

"Emerson! Dear girl, I'm up fifty and Lutz is seething. Sure you won't sit in for a hand?"

"No, Berlin, thanks anyway. Got to get going soon. Going to Grover's Corner in the morning."

"Okay, honey. Good to see you," Berlin said, slapping her on the back and smiling broadly.

They took their plates to the kitchen, lingering a bit.

"Got to go?" Hope asked.

"Yeah," Emerson said, shyly.

"Can I walk you out?" Hope asked.

"Sure," Emerson said.

Emerson thanked Katherine for dinner and made her excuses at the poker table, the raucousness growing ever louder. Rachel winked at Hope. Beer bottles were everywhere, and cigar smoke was so thick it made Hope's eyes water.

Hope and Emerson stood out on the porch, suddenly embarrassed to be alone together.

"Thanks for coming," Hope said.

"Thanks for making me," Emerson said. "So . . ." Emerson said, rocking on her heels, her hands in her pocket. "You and Rachel want to come by and see the studio? Maybe we could go to lunch. I'll be back by then, you know, if you don't have other plans."

"Where was the studio? They say you live in it," Hope asked, thinking she hadn't seen any work when she was scooting about Emerson's third floor without walls.

"It's on the fourth floor."

"What, you own the whole disastrous building?" Hope chided.

"Yep. It's a pit, but it's home," Emerson said, smiling.

"I'd love to, Emerson. Good night," Hope said.

"Good night, my pretty little friend," Emerson said, turning around to walk off into the crisp summer evening. Hope stood for a moment watching her, feeling weird things, not knowing what they were exactly.

Hope was drained, and she told Katherine she was off to bed. Katherine smiled at her.

"You did good tonight, Hope. Someone's got to reach Emerson, and that someone might be you."

Hope looked at her, puzzled.

"Good night, sweetheart," Katherine said, kissing her forehead.

Hope smiled as she climbed the stairs to the dormer room she shared with Rachel. What a nice family, she thought as she brushed her teeth, studying her reflection for a moment in the old, beveled mirror. What did they see that she didn't? Hope saw a young woman who looked frazzled, bent, and scared. How could she possibly help someone else when she was so hopelessly lost?

"They'll fall in love, mark my words," Berlin told Rachel and Katherine as they stood in the kitchen finishing off the last vestiges of the blueberry pie.

"You've got blueberry all over your lips, Berlin," Katherine said.

"Kiss it off," Berlin said, puckering up.

Katherine obliged her. They'd be in each other's arms before morning. Thank god that their room was at the opposite end of the house, Rachel thought. It was the last thing Hope needed to hear. Berlin was loud, and her mother wasn't the quietest lover, either. Rachel remembered coming into their room when she was a child to find the two of them, not fucking but wrapped up in each other's arms.

Her two mommies. Berlin wasn't really a mother so much as an adviser-friend. Rachel never called her mother, and Berlin didn't expect it. She'd let Katherine deal with issues of child raising. Berlin was always the one who smoothed ruffled feathers, kissed skinned knees, and brought the two of them, Rachel and her mother, back together after one of their head-butting, hair-pulling, screaming arguments.

Rachel stood staring at them, thinking.

"You mean Hope and Emerson?" Rachel said, rather stunned by Berlin's prediction.

"Why of course, dear. Who else?" Berlin said, peeking out from behind Katherine, who was dancing with her lover slowly, prepping, reminding, anticipating. Rachel hoped when she found her soul mate that they'd be as good together as Katherine and Berlin. They'd been deeply in love for as long as Rachel could remember.

"But Hope has a girlfriend," Rachel said.

"Since when has that ever stopped anyone?" Katherine said.

"It's stopped me," Berlin said.

"That's only because you've always been madly in love with me," Katherine said, smiling and pinching Berlin's buns.

"It's true. I am madly in love with you."

"After all these years?" Berlin said coyly.

"Of course."

"Besides, when you meet the one you've spent your whole life waiting for, girlfriends don't count for much. People have thrown more to the wind than a mere girlfriend," Berlin said.

"Duke of Windsor, for example," Katherine said.

"God, you're good," Berlin said. She had taught Katherine everything she knew about British history. If Berlin's mother hated the mother country, Berlin had an ongoing love affair with merry old England.

"So Pamela is a mere girlfriend and Emerson is Hope's true love? Berlin, I don't think Hope has been looking for anyone her whole life. She can't even find herself," Rachel said, raising a skeptical eyebrow.

"Oh, darling, there are still things I obviously have to teach you. We oftentimes don't know that we're looking or that we've even lost it. The *it* manifests itself in other things, like not being happy and not knowing why. Not taking care of yourself, like both Hope and Emerson. By missing something but not being able to put your finger on it, a something that aches inside you and no matter what you do it won't go away. You can't drink it away or drown it away or run it away. It sits like a lump in your heart until that person walks into your life and saves you. Those two will save each other, believe me," Berlin said, shaking her head. She looked at Katherine. "Woman, take me to bed and make me want!"

They left Rachel standing there pondering. She could hear them clambering up the stairs, laughing and giggling like two schoolgirls.

Rachel followed shortly after. When she got to her room she found Hope lying there.

"You're not sleeping," Rachel admonished.

Hope leaned up on one elbow. "I was kind of dozing," she offered.

"Until you heard my mom and Berlin. Sorry."

"It's okay, really. I do feel better, Rachel. I think this is going to work out."

"I'm glad. I'm glad you came."

Rachel got undressed. Hope lay back down, drawing the covers up around her neck like when she was a little girl.

In the dark, Hope asked, "Rachel, did anyone think it was funny that you grew up in a lesbian household and that you're a lesbian?"

"You mean, like having two lesbian mothers condition me to become a lesbian?"

"Well, yeah," Hope said. She'd been pondering the question all day.

"Not here, necessarily, but it did get asked in New York. I dated this psych major once who wanted to turn our family into her thesis. No, it never occurred to me. I've always had an attraction to women. I didn't have to go through that whole playing straight thing because I already knew I was gay. I fell in love with Emerson, and my sexual initiation began. It was that simple."

Hope nearly fell out of bed. "You and Emerson!"

"Why is that so hard to believe?" Rachel asked.

"I don't know. Emerson seems unobtainable, dangerous, I guess, and definitely not your type."

"What's my type?" Rachel asked. "Perhaps with your insight I'll find my perfect love twin and we'll live happily ever after."

"Don't be snide. I think you like more demur tamer women. You seem to be more the hunter than the fox."

"Basically you're saying I like boring, safe women. Thanks."

"No, but Emerson seems like she would have been a handful, and you like lower maintenance women."

"And Emerson's high maintenance?"

"Yes," Hope answered.

"You're right, but I don't think I'll ever love anyone the way I loved her. Sometimes it seems everyone is granted one great love of her life — whether she gets to spend the rest of her life with her is another question — but she loves one person more anyone else. Emerson, I think, is my one," Rachel said, looking up at the ceiling.

"What happened?"

"Angel happened. She walked into Emerson's life and never left it. Still haunts her to this day."

"Where is Angel now?"

"The convent in Grover's Corner."

"She's a nun?" Hope said.

"You've heard of lesbian nuns."

"Yes, but don't they usually run away from convents?"

"This lesbian ran into one, which is another long

and sordid story. Anyway, Emerson's never been the same since."

"That's sad," Hope said.

"It is sad. Hope, is Pamela the one great love of your life?"

"No, she's not. I love Pamela, but there's always been something not quite right between us. But she'll do, I suppose. I think if I learned to be more assertive and she learned to calm down we might make a go of it. I'm not ready to give up."

"That's good."

"Why good?" Hope asked, confused by Rachel's response. Rachel wasn't fond of Pamela and had offered Hope refuge on more than one occasion if she wanted to leave Pamela.

"Because you're my friend, and I want you to be happy and not get hurt."

"Who would hurt me?"

"I don't know. You get some sleep," Rachel said.

"Rachel?" Hope called out into the darkness.

"Yes?"

"You don't think you and Emerson could patch things up?"

"No, darling, we're long past that. Christ, we were sixteen when we fell in love. We were babies really. Been through too much now to be lovers. We'll always be friends. Besides, you just said she was too high maintenance."

"I know, but I want you to find someone nice to love."

"Someday," Rachel said, thinking I do love someone nice, but unfortunately all the nice ones are taken.

Rachel lay awake thinking about the first time she made love with Emerson. Sweet sixteen and never been kissed. Emerson had been a demon then, but fun. Rachel had never had such fun. Emerson used to drive her father crazy. That was how she ended up in genteel Southern boarding schools.

He couldn't control her; neither could anyone else. He wanted the best things for Emerson and had the money to do it. He sent her to private school after private school, all of which she got thrown out of for various violations. Finally when she was sixteen she came home, promised to be good, and went to public school with the rest of the townies.

Katherine had told Jack Emerson his daughter was being naughty because she wanted to come home. When he finally let her, she was good. But she was also the one thing he didn't want her to be: a lesbian. That was why he had sent her away, hoping by not living in Heroy she would grow up with normal tastes. She didn't.

The last school she got thrown out of for sleeping with another girl. The headmistress found them together, arms and legs wrapped around each other. Emerson wouldn't denounce what had happened, and the school was forced to expel her. Jack Emerson gave up. Emerson did what she pleased. He still loved her dearly, but he stopped trying to make her something she wasn't. He let Katherine take over the rest of her upbringing.

And that was how Rachel and Emerson took to hanging around each other. Katherine thought it would be a good idea if Rachel, who was fairly well behaved, socialized Emerson. Katherine hoped it would get rid of Emerson's rough edges. What Katherine didn't count on was the two of them falling in love.

But how could Rachel not fall in love with Emerson, who was worldly, experienced, wild, and beautiful. Rachel was head over heels in love before she knew it. She remembered the first time Emerson kissed her. They were sitting out behind McNeely's barn, their backs up against a haystack, drinking a bottle of strawberry wine, awful stuff. Emerson looked over at her with those incredible blue eyes and said, "You know what I'd really like to do?"

Rachel, like a dumb ass, said, "What?"

"I'd really like to kiss you."

Emerson leaned over and gently kissed her, and then kissed her again. She kissed her neck and reached for her breast, taking it in her mouth. Rachel had never felt anything like it. Emerson took her places she'd never been, and when it was over, she held her, worrying that she may have hurt her. Rachel lay naked, her head on Emerson's chest, certain she was experiencing the happiest moment of her young life. From that moment forward, all Rachel thought about was Emerson, how she felt, how she tasted, how she smelled, every curve of her body.

Her mother found them together in Rachel's twin bed dead asleep after a long night of lovemaking. Emerson was between Rachel's legs, asleep on her stomach. Katherine was furious. Berlin was ecstatic. There was a huge argument in the kitchen.

"My little girl's not a little girl anymore," Berlin

said, hugging Rachel. Her mother slammed down Rachel's plate of eggs and glared at her. Rachel knew something big was about to unfold.

"I wanted you to make her into a lady, not sleep with her," her mother finally burst out.

Rachel choked on her coffee. It took several moments with Berlin patting her on the back to regain her composure.

"What?"

"Don't you What me, young lady. I saw you this morning," Katherine belted out.

"I don't understand why you're so mad. I thought you liked Emerson," Rachel said, looking at Berlin for help.

"Have you really thought about this?"

"Thought about what?" Rachel asked her mother.

"About the social connotations here."

"What social connotations?" Rachel asked stupidly.

"That sleeping with a woman makes you a lesbian," Katherine said, hands on her hips.

"So?" Rachel said.

"Is that what you really want to be?" Katherine said.

"What's wrong with it? You're one."

"But maybe I didn't want you to be one," Katherine said between gritted teeth.

"This is just great. You're a lesbian, so I can't be one, is that it?" Rachel said, getting up from the table. "What would people think? That you turned me into one? Christ, in Heroy who cares?"

"Maybe you won't always live in Heroy," Katherine yelled back as Rachel thumped up the stairs.

"Can't hear you," Rachel yelled back.

Katherine started for her, but Berlin grabbed her arm. "Let her go."

Katherine glared at Berlin but acquiesced.

Berlin's solution to the problem was to buy a Rachel a double bed. Rachel came home from school to find her room filled with a beautiful wrought-iron bed with a giant red bow tied in the middle of it.

Katherine grew less hostile. Berlin counseled her.

"Would you rather she was out giving a town boy, Dickie Sharpe for example, a blow job, ending up pregnant, someone's wife, with dead eyes and thwarted aspirations?" Berlin said.

"Not all straight couples are like that, Berlin," Katherine said.

"I would think you'd be happy that she grew up to be a lesbian."

"Why? So she can go through life being a pervert? Not everyplace is like Heroy. We've been other places. You know what it's like. Rachel's been lucky so far. What's going to happen when she goes off to college?"

"Oh, my, nothing quite like all those coeds in tight sweaters," Berlin said, thinking back to younger days.

"You're absolutely hopeless!"

"She'll have a good time. She'll meet other lesbians, fuck her brains out, and learn a lot about herself. Times have changed, Katherine. Things aren't as hard as they used to be."

"I know. I worry about her. I don't want her to get hurt."

"Getting hurt is part of growing up. Rachel's a big girl now."

And then it dawned on Berlin why Katherine was

having such a difficult time. It wasn't so much that her daughter was a lesbian as it was that her daughter was in love with Emerson. Katherine had been in love with Emerson's mother.

Berlin took Rachel aside and explained what happened over Cokes at the café while Katherine was out.

"You mean those two boinked?" Rachel had asked.

"In those days it was more like a heated friendship, but Sarah wanted a family, wanted to be married. It was very hard on Katherine letting go. And then when Sarah died giving birth to Emerson, that just about sent everyone around the bend," Berlin told her, thinking about the last time she had seen Sarah alive. She and Katherine had lain on either side of Sarah, gently rubbing her big belly and trying to imagine the tiny one inside.

"And then you had me. Tell me that story," Rachel begged.

"Naw, that's another long story. Some other day. Shh, here comes your mother. So I want you to be nice to her and try to understand where she is coming from."

"But I still don't get it. She loved Emerson's mother, so I'm not supposed to love Emerson."

"No, it's just that it reminds her of things that hurt her. When you're older you'll understand the pain that the past can give. Until then, take my word for it. Now promise to be nice?"

"I promise to be nice. And can I have Emerson over to spend the night in the new bed?"

"You two are insatiable. Yes, but quietly," Berlin said, thinking of her insatiable days and then laughing at herself. She was still insatiable. Who was she trying to fool?

Berlin still hadn't told her the story of how she came into the world, Rachel thought sleepily. Someday she'd make her tell.

Five

Hope and Rachel scrambled up the four flights of stairs to find Emerson sweating profusely and moving crates.

"Perfect timing. Still a couple more trips," Emerson said, smiling.

"Great. You invite us over for lunch, but you're going to make us work first," Rachel said smugly.

"Rach, c'mon. This shit's heavy and I'm tired," Emerson pleaded.

"Should have bought a building with an elevator," Rachel said.

"It has an elevator; it just doesn't work," Emerson said.

"Should put the studio on the first floor then," Rachel said.

"I can't. The light's bad, and it gives me claustrophobia."

"Do you really suffer from claustrophobia?" Hope asked.

"She never used to until she was forced to spend three days in tight quarters," Rachel explained.

"Where was that?" Hope asked, trying to imagine what kind of tight quarters. "Let me guess. Another long story I'm not going to hear."

Emerson stood looking at her for a moment, studying.

"No, I'll give you the abridged version. I went bonkers one night, and instead of hauling me off to jail they thought the sanitarium would be nicer. Well, it wasn't nicer. They put me in a very small, very quiet, very dark room where it took everything I had not to go crazier than I already was. In fact, if it hadn't been for Lutz Lasbeer's rather prodigious influence, I might still be there," Emerson said.

"I'm sorry," Hope said, wishing she hadn't pried.

"Don't be. By the end of the summer you'll know every sordid detail about everyone."

"This, of course, includes you," Emerson said over her shoulder as the three of them tromped downstairs and finished loading whatever it was Emerson had delivered.

Emerson and Rachel lifted up either end of a large crate.

Rachel looked over at her. "Still think about it?"

"Still think, smell, dream about it. Sometimes I

feel like I can't breathe. I work nights to get away from the nightmares," Emerson replied.

It was enough to give anyone nightmares. Emerson outside the convent, screaming and crying, demanding to see her wife, talk to her. The mother superior telling her that Angel was married to God now and that what she had done with Emerson was a sin not a marriage. Emerson lunging at the nun and being hauled off by the police. Then three days of hell, not knowing anything, just sitting and rocking and crying herself to sleep until the door opened and Lutz stood there, a massive figure with the light behind her. Emerson squinting to see her, thinking she was hallucinating. Lutz getting her out of there and taking her home to Katherine.

Emerson gave up harassing the convent but took to drink and then nearly drowned in the pond. Now she maintained an even, although stunted, keel through the backwater of her brokenhearted memories. Both Rachel and Emerson knew that something had broken, and neither one of them seemed able to fix it.

Hope stood in front of one of the sculptures.

"These women are incredible," Hope said, studying the figures.

She sat down on a bench next to one, a woman doubled over with grief, her whole body racked with the pain of it, cast in bronze. It was an impressive effort at capturing human despair. Hope put her arm around her as if in consolation. Rachel and Emerson stared at her mortified.

"What, I'm not supposed to touch them?" Hope asked, quickly removing her arm.

"No, you can touch her. That one just has special significance," Emerson explained. It was the last sculpture she had done of Angel, and it held all the anguish they both felt for a love affair gone wrong. Her agent, Lauren, kept trying to sell it. Emerson refused.

"Actually, that's just what she needed," Emerson said.

"I'm sorry," Hope said.

"Don't be. That's another story that I'll tell you over lunch, and you can tell me all about the girlfriend you ran away from. Deal?" Emerson said.

"You *are* going to change your shirt before we go," Rachel said, surveying Emerson's dirty front.

"I hadn't planned on it," Emerson replied, remedying the situation by brushing it off.

"Well, you are. Put something decent on; we're going out for lunch."

"I didn't realize the café was considered a high-fashion lunch," Emerson said, rummaging around for a new shirt. The holey one she put on was not an improvement.

"Christ, don't you have something better than that? The thing should be a rag," Rachel said, rummaging herself.

"You gave me this shirt," Emerson said, looking hurt.

"Eons ago. What happened to you? You used to be so fashionable, downright spiffy," Rachel admonished.

Emerson looked over at Hope and made faces, mimicking Rachel.

Hope laughed.

"You're such a brat," Rachel said, coming up with a decent shirt.

"I'm going to make Hope take you shopping. She has good taste, and you definitely need some new clothes. I can't believe Lauren lets you get away with this stuff. What do you do about shows?"

"She won't let me come anymore. She's says I'm rude," Emerson replied.

"I find that hard to believe," Rachel chided.

Emerson looked over at Hope. "Rachel does this every summer. She tries to reform me, but what she doesn't know is that the minute she leaves I go right back to my old wicked ways."

"I know you do, but at least I don't have to see it," Rachel said.

They went to the café where Berlin and the tent dykes were playing five-card stud. As usual, Berlin was winning.

"C'mon in girls. Meet my new friends — Amy, Charlene, Denise, and Lily."

Looks flashed between both groups of young women. Emerson muttered hello and went off in search of Katherine.

After Hope and Rachel seated themselves, Hope asked, "Is Emerson always that rude in a crowd?"

"She has an aversion to lesbians," Rachel said flatly.

"Isn't she one?" Hope asked, confused.

"Yes, but that doesn't mean she likes them."

"I don't understand."

"Emerson has given up on women. After breaking

my heart and then having her own heart broken, Emerson has not been one for love. And the funny part is that being an artist seems to attract a lot of women, but Emerson won't have a one of them. Shit, I wish I could generate that much traffic. I think she comes across as cold so she won't have to deal with them. Of course, that seems to attract them too. You watch."

"Your mother is an incredible cook," Emerson said, returning from the kitchen holding a half-eaten piece of cherry pie.

"You're supposed to wait," Rachel admonished.

"Never was one for rules," Emerson said.

"Don't we know."

After lunch over coffee and pie, Emerson told Hope about Angel. Rachel filled in the details that Emerson had been too drunk to recall.

"There, end of story, end of my life with women," Emerson said, rather pleased for getting it off her chest. She had never told anyone the story. It felt good to say the words, like letting go of them. The images became strangely light, almost like they belonged to someone else's past. Melodramatic enough to have become humorous.

"You know, Rach, I never thought I'd laugh about those times. Maybe I am getting better," Emerson said.

"I wouldn't go that far. If we could get you to go out with someone that would be getting better," Rachel said.

"There's nothing wrong with spending your life alone. Sometimes I think it's better. I'm not the nicest person to be around. This way I don't hurt anyone, and no one hurts me."

49

"You like it safe," Rachel said.

"Safe is better than chaotic. I can't create things when my life is in a state of upheaval. That's all love is to me, mountaintop and then abyss."

"What if you could find someone nice, someone who didn't torment you, who would be an attribute to your life, who would help take care of you and be nice, supporting, neither a doormat nor a tyrant — would you then share your life with her?" Rachel asked.

"No," Emerson replied flatly

"Why not?"

"Because there is no one like that, especially a woman."

"You're a cynic," Rachel said.

"No, facts prove me correct. Do you have someone like that? No. Even your pretty little friend can't find it, and she seems awfully nice. Let me guess. You're the doormat and she's the tyrant. You can't stand it, so you leave. And is it really going to be any better when you get back? No. There is nothing good about love," Emerson said.

"What about Mom and Berlin?" Rachel said.

"Fluke, pure and simple."

"There are other couples in this town who are happy," Rachel said.

"No, not happy. They tolerate each other."

And as if to prove Emerson right, Sal and Elise came flying through the café door, one trailing the other in hot pursuit.

"Goddammit, stop following me," Sal said through gritted teeth.

"I'm not following you. I'm trying to talk to you," Elise replied, as they both took a seat at the counter.

"Coffee, please," Elise said, smiling at Katherine, trying to pretend everything was all right.

"Another happy, loving couple," Emerson said. "See, the larger one, Sal, she's the tyrant, and Elise, the smaller, more attractive one, she's the doormat. Sal doesn't treat her very well, but every time it looks like Elise might have found herself someone else, Sal kicks into gear and wins her back. Remember the time Sal chained everything they owned down because Elise had taken up with Ruthie Clark?" Emerson said.

"Yeah," Rachel said, chuckling.

"Sal literally chained everything they owned together and locked it up because she refused to let Elise have anything if Ruthie Clark was going to use it. Sal hates Ruthie Clark because Elise and Ruthie go way back. They should have married instead of Sal and Elise," Emerson said.

"It probably would have worked out better," Rachel said.

The conversation at the counter was growing more heated.

Katherine rolled her eyes at them.

"What's wrong this time?" Rachel asked.

"The same old thing, I suppose. I'm sure if we sit here long enough we'll find out," Emerson said.

Katherine brought them over beers, courtesy of the tent dykes.

"Oh god, here we go again," Emerson said, setting hers in front of Hope. "I can see the headlines now, NEW DYKES IN TOWN CRUISE LOCALS, LOOKING FOR A LITTLE SUMMERTIME FUN," Emerson said, disgust clouding her face.

"Look, I know you're sleeping with her. Don't lie

to me!" Sal screamed, unable to contain her rage a moment longer.

"I'm not sleeping with her. We're just friends," Elise responded equally as loud.

Emerson got up abruptly. "I've had more than enough of this shit for one day!"

Hope and Rachel looked stunned.

Emerson walked over to Sal and Elise. "You know what, Sal, she'd probably sleep with you if you weren't such a cunt. Elise, you really need to stop lying. You've been in love with Ruthie for as long as I can remember, and I've seen you two slinking around late at night. You need to make a decision. And stick to it." Emerson let the café door slam behind her. Everyone in the café watched her go.

"I'm going to fucking kill her," Sal said, getting up off her stool and making for the door.

"Oh no you're not," Katherine said, blocking the doorway. "She's the only one in this town with the balls to call it what it is. Lay one hand on Emerson and you'll live to regret it."

Sal sat back down. Katherine poured her another cup of coffee.

Hope looked over at Rachel. "Oh my."

"Yeah, welcome to Heroy," Rachel said.

Hope went to bed that night thinking Emerson was the most beautiful savage she'd ever met.

It was afternoon, and Hope was lying on the balustrade of the porch dozing with a book across her stomach. She half heard some sort of scraping noise on the sidewalk.

Emerson looked at Hope as she lay there, studying the curve of her legs, which were turning light brown with summer's touch, studying the curve of her neck and the soft round line of her shoulder. It was times like these she wished she had her sketch pad; her fingers fairly itched with the desire. Maybe she could convince Hope to pose for her. She instantly doubted she'd ever convince such a ladylike creature to get naked for the sake of art.

She clunked up the stairs to the house. Hope opened an eye, peering out to see who it was.

"Must be a great book; it put you to sleep," Emerson said, smiling.

Hope laughed. "Actually, Pamela wrote it. It's one of her feminist pieces. I've been meaning to read it and see just what kind of a mind my girlfriend has."

"She's more like your wife, isn't she?"

"I guess you could say that," Hope said, sitting up.

"How long have you two been together?" Emerson said, snatching up the book to see the title.

"Three years."

Emerson flipped the book over. On the back was a picture of Pamela Severson, a tall woman, light-colored eyes, dark hair, intelligent looking.

"She's an attractive woman," Emerson said.

"And rather formidable," Hope replied.

"Look, I'm sorry about the other day. I'm rude, but I can't seem to help myself," Emerson said shyly. She sat down and unlaced her skates, pulling them off to stretch her ankles.

Hope sat down next to her and picked up a skate, spinning the wheels. She looked over at Emerson, arching an eyebrow. "These are fun, aren't they?"

"What? Mom won't let you try them because they're dangerous?" Emerson chided.

Hope blushed.

"I'm sorry. They're not that bad if you wear knee pads and a helmet."

"Which you don't."

"But I'm self-destructive and you're not."

"I wouldn't be so sure about that."

"I could teach you, and Pamela would never have to know," Emerson offered.

Hope smiled. "It wouldn't hurt to try them, now would it?"

"No. How about tomorrow?"

"Wonderful," Hope said, spinning the wheels again and imagining herself moving quickly across the pavement.

"Why were you so angry the other day?" Hope asked, suddenly remembering why Emerson had come by.

"It's that whole love thing. Everybody's got to have it and yet everybody's miserable in it. I mean, why bother? But people try to set you up on dates, like Berlin the other afternoon. She told those women that we were more or less available. I don't want to be someone's summertime fling, and that's all they want. I don't understand what's wrong with being alone, with wanting to be alone."

"Humans are companionable creatures, and love does have its nice touches."

"Which turn nasty just as quick. The good part of love never lasts. I'd rather be nasty to myself than hurt someone else. When you're alone you can do that."

"And from what I've heard, that's all you've been doing to yourself."

"I'm working on it. You don't have much room to talk. Look what being in love has done for you. There were more nasty moments than nice ones, weren't there?"

Hope studied her hands. Her long fingers used to make Pamela ache with longing just looking at them, remembering how they felt as they caressed her body. That had changed, and they didn't really have the time or the energy for love anymore. It was always hurried love, quick-fix love. Hope hated that.

Emerson broke the spell, picking up one of Hope's idle hands and examining it.

"You have beautiful hands. If I teach you to skate, will you let me sculpt your hands?"

Hope hesitated. "I guess that's fair."

"So, you never answered my question. How good is your love? I mean, you're here and she's not. If you were my true love, I would never let you stray so far. I couldn't bear it. I'd miss you too much."

"But maybe I'm not a very good partner," Hope said, meeting Emerson's gaze. Blue eyes to blue eyes.

"No, I'll bet you're good. You care about things. You care too much to be bad. You don't play around, do you?"

"No. I've been tempted, but I never have."

"I used to play around. Used to play around on Rachel and played around on Angel in the beginning, but not after we came here. I was good then. It's a mean thing to do. See, I'm no good at love. Best to stay out of it."

"Emerson, how old are you?"

"Thirty-two."

"That's awfully young to throw in the towel. I mean, that's like those women who are widowed young and never remarry. You deny yourself a second chance at happiness."

"Look at my role models. You saw how Elise and Sal are, and the town is full of others like them. I don't want to be like that."

"Maybe you just haven't found the right one. Maybe Elise should marry Ruthie Clark; maybe everyone would be happier. I think sometimes we end up with the wrong people and that's why we're so nasty to each other, because deep down we know we're not where we're supposed to be. We're inhibiting each other's search. But it's hard to let go, to admit to the failure."

"Is that where you're at?"

Hope looked over at her. "Probably."

"So Pamela's not the right one?"

"Deep down, no."

"But she'll do."

"Yes."

"Why are you settling after you just said we should try to find the right ones?"

"Because it's easy to give advice and much harder to live by it."

"Here's a deal for you. I'll believe in love again if and when you find the right woman to love," Emerson said.

"How can I make a deal like that?" Hope said.

"Very easily. You say, Emerson, it's a deal."

Hope smiled.

"I'll take that as a yes. I'm coming by tomorrow and we'll skate," Emerson said, putting her skates back on and whirling off the porch.

Rachel walked out into the morning light, holding a cup of coffee and reaching for her sunglasses.

"What the hell?" she said, looking down onto the sidewalk to find Emerson holding Hope's hands and easing her forward on a pair of skates. Hope was decked out in elbow and knee pads, gloves, and a helmet.

"Emerson's teaching me to skate," Hope said, her face flushed with excitement.

"I can see that," Rachel said, smiling.

"She bought me my very own skates," Hope said, smiling appreciatively at Emerson, who had immediately trotted off to Grover's Corner the day before and bought skates. Emerson was sneaky. She made Berlin go upstairs and find out what shoe size Hope wore so she'd get the right ones. She wanted everything to be perfect. She didn't know why exactly. It just had to be.

The look on Hope's face made it all worthwhile. She looked like a kid that got exactly what she wanted for Christmas. Emerson was ecstatic.

"Oh great. Now we'll have two menaces around town. And what's with the helmet?" Rachel said, tapping the one on Emerson's head.

"Well, I couldn't make her wear one if I wasn't willing to. I saw Pamela's picture yesterday; she doesn't look like a woman that would take it kindly if I sent her girlfriend back as damaged goods," Emerson said.

Hope smiled.

"Well, be careful, and please don't teach her to jump over fire hydrants. I hate when you do that," Rachel said.

Rachel watched as Emerson showed Hope what to do, and they teetered off together in the direction of the courthouse, which had a large smooth plaza and steps that Emerson loved to jump. Rachel prayed Emerson wouldn't teach Hope that either.

Rachel went back to the kitchen to get more coffee. She found Berlin in there going over her racing forms and drinking a Coke.

"How can you drink that stuff in the morning?" Rachel said.

"Same way you drink that stuff," Berlin said, pointing at Rachel's coffee mug.

"Did you see Emerson and Hope this morning?" Rachel asked, still puzzled by the whole event.

"Yeah, cute aren't they?" Berlin said smiling.

"Emerson was downright considerate. Nice, even."

"I told you those two are going to fall in love," Berlin said, shaking her head and folding up her form.

"No, I still think you're off base on that one. But friends. They'd be good for each other."

"Let's have a wager, shall we? Say a twenty spot that those two get together."

"You're compulsive, but you're on," Rachel said, shaking Berlin's outstretched hand.

"I may be compulsive, but I'm also extremely successful. You wait until you get the little annuity I have set up for you and you'll see just how successful."

"You put your gambling money away for me?" Rachel asked. This was the first time she'd ever heard of it.

"Yes. I want you to get a house and a good start in life when you finish school. I gamble with purpose. You'll see," Berlin said, putting her arm around Rachel.

Six

Hope, Rachel, and Katherine were going to Grover's Corner to do some shopping. The phone rang, and Berlin answered it. The call was for Hope. Slightly puzzled, Hope picked up the phone. A familiar voice came whirling across it.

Rachel and Katherine waited patiently while Hope tried to explain to Pamela that they were on their way out the door. It didn't work. Pamela wanted to talk now, and now it would be. Hope shrugged her shoulders and motioned them on. They left her standing in the hallway with her head against the wall. Story of her life.

Rachel let out a jagged breath and looked over at her mother. "I hate that woman. She does shit like this to Hope all the time. Drop everything you're doing, honey, I'm ready to be entertained now. It's like Hope isn't allowed to have an existence outside of the one Pamela has planned for her."

"Now, Hope," Pamela was saying, "I know you wanted to spend the whole summer, but you simply must take this class from Irene. It's a must. Besides, it's second session, and that still leaves you four more weeks of vacation and then you start back early. Come on. I miss you."

"I don't know Pamela. I didn't plan on school this summer."

"Look, I'll register you and you can think on it. But I really want you to take this, and if you're willing to take a second class, you'll graduate in time for McAllister's retirement, which would be perfect. I know I could squeeze you onto the faculty, with little or no trouble. It'll be perfect."

Hope had a stomachache by the time Pamela was through. All those same weird feelings of anxiety came flooding back. She needed Rachel, and Rachel wouldn't be back for hours. She went to find Berlin. She ended up sitting across the table from Emerson, who was slumped over asleep on the table with a blanket draped over her shoulders.

"What's wrong with her?" Hope asked.

"Nightmares again. She works all night to get away from them, comes in here for coffee, and falls asleep halfway through," Berlin told her.

Emerson's fingers were still wrapped around the cup.

"You okay, honey?" Berlin asked, noticing how pale Hope looked.

Before Hope could answer, the buzzer to the back door rang.

"Damn, it's the produce driver. Have I got a few choice words for him. Slugs in the lettuce to begin with. Grab a cup of coffee. I'll be right back."

Hope sat watching Emerson, remembering the afternoon they went skating. Remembering how Emerson intently listened to Hope's stories, her eyes never straying from Hope's face when they sat down to rest in the park. It was nothing like Pamela's divided attention. Emerson made Hope feel like she mattered. When Emerson spoke, she only looked up occasionally to catch Hope's gaze, too shy to make direct contact. Hope told her things that Pamela never knew, never took the time to know. And Hope knew Emerson spoke of things long buried. That afternoon they became friends.

The day seemed to fly by, and before they knew it darkness set in. They had dinner at Katherine's. The kitchen was cozy with the warm breath of summer blowing gently through the open windows. Food and laughter. Emerson's quirky smile and Katherine's shining eyes, glad to see her worrisome children having a good time. Emerson and Hope lingered a moment saying good night, like things were beginning to happen between them. Hope lay in bed replaying the whole wonderful day. She remembered feeling good, hungry for things she'd almost forgot about.

Emerson stirred, and a ringlet fell into her coffee. Hope gingerly plucked it out, holding it for a moment. It was thick and soft. She loved Emerson's hair, wavy and unruly. She imagined running her fingers through it. She thought about washing it. If hair could be erotic, Emerson's was. Hope blushed to herself. She let the curl drop. Emerson opened her eyes and tried to focus. She rubbed them, looked around for a moment to get her bearings.

"Ah, yes, sleeping in the café again. My pretty little friend, what are you doing? I wasn't being a very good coffee companion. You should have woke me. Shit! What time is it?" Emerson said, looking outside and noticing the sun.

Hope looked at her watch. "Ten-thirty."

"Late, late, late for a very important date," Emerson said, getting up abruptly. Then she looked at Hope.

"Come with me. You can meet my agent, Lauren, dragon lady extraordinaire," Emerson said, grabbing Hope's hand and whisking her across the street to the studio.

Lauren was already there, pacing back and forth and smoking a long, dark cigarette. She was dressed in a black, fashionably tailored suit. She quickly appraised Hope.

"Dammit, Emerson, you'll be late for your own funeral."

"Actually, if it wasn't for my pretty little friend here, I would be really late, still catnapping at the café."

"Does your friend have a name?"

"Hope Kaznot," Hope said, extending her hand. She wondered if Emerson remembered her name. Not that it really mattered. They seemed to be getting on fine without it.

Emerson took them both on a tour of her latest work, which was scheduled to open in late August. Lauren seemed pleased with Emerson's progress, but Hope felt like she was being sized up as impediment or muse.

After Lauren left, Emerson let out a sigh of relief.

"Free for another two months," she said, pulling out a Coke from the fridge. "Hey, you want a scotch? I've still got the bottle. You look like you might need one. Lauren didn't put you off, did she? She's a bit much at times, but she sells a lot of artwork, so we all put up with her New York bitchiness. Are you all right?"

Hope sat down. "I will take that scotch."

Emerson promptly got it for her and then sat next to her on the ratty couch.

"What's wrong?" Emerson said, looking over at her intently.

"Pamela called."

"Oh," Emerson said, rolling her tongue over her upper lip, trying to ascertain what this meant.

"She wants me to come back for the second summer session and to take a class I'm not interested in so I can graduate earlier and take a teaching position I have no desire to have," Hope blurted out, immediately apologizing. "I didn't mean to make it sound that way."

"No, I think you did," Emerson said, getting up to refill Hope's glass.

Hope looked up at her. "I did." Then she laughed.

Emerson smiled. "I love you way you laugh."

"One of my few positive attributes," Hope said wryly.

"Why do you say that? You're so hard on yourself. You're wonderful. Why don't you know that?"

"No, I'm worthless, and I'm even more worthless if I don't get my doctorate and teach."

"Why should you do things you don't want to?"

"Because I'm supposed to," Hope said, letting out a sigh of resignation.

"Says who? Pamela?"

"And my mother, who thinks that if I absolutely must be a lesbian the least I could do is to have a decent profession. And the thing is, it doesn't really matter. Next year I get my trust fund. It's not like I have to be something that makes a lot of money."

"So it's a prestige thing?" Emerson queried.

"I suppose."

"What do you want?"

Hope looked over at her. "Promise you won't laugh if I tell you."

Emerson looked puzzled. "Is it that bad?"

"No. I don't think so. It's rather ordinary. I just want to be happily married. You know, make dinner, have a garden, live out somewhere, take care of someone."

"And that someone isn't Pamela?"

"No, she's not like that. She wants an intellectual accompanist, someone she can brag about as the mortal fit to be her mate. I'll never live up to her expectations."

"Is that why you left?"

"Yes."

"And that's why you're not ready to go back."

"Yes."

"Tell her to piss off. You'll come home when you're ready."

"Oh, Emerson, it's not that easy."

"Yes it is. You simply say, Pamela I am not fit to come back yet. Do not make me and do not expect me. See, simple," Emerson said, getting up and going over to a wood cupboard. She pulled an ancient office telephone from its depths and went in search of an outlet.

"I know there's one here somewhere."

"Emerson what are you doing?" Hope asked, alarmed.

"You're going to call Pamela," Emerson replied, moving a heap of dusty canvas. "Ah, there it is."

"I can't do that," Hope said, nervously pouring herself another drink.

"You can't let her intimidate you. Now, what's the number?" Emerson asked, finger poised.

Hope sat mute.

"Look you can either give me the number or I'll dial assistance."

Hope, against her better judgment, gave her the number. Emerson dialed. Pamela answered. Emerson handed the phone to Hope, who was now in a panic. She refused to take it.

Hope could hear multiple hellos.

"Pamela, this is Emerson Wells, a friend of your girlfriend. Look, she's not coming home until fall semester. She turned green just at the thought of it. So give her a call back in, say, late August."

"What!" Pamela shrieked. "Is Hope there? Let me talk to her right now."

Emerson pulled the phone away and put her hand over the receiver. "She wants to talk to you."

Hope covered her face with her hands. "Oh, Emerson, I can't believe you just did that."

"Well, I got it started. Now you finish it. You can do it. I know you can."

Hope looked at Emerson for a moment, thinking, I'm not ready to leave yet. I haven't combed your hair. I haven't learned to jump on skates, and you haven't sculpted my hands. She picked up the phone.

"Hope, what is going on? And who is that woman?"

"She's a friend, a concerned friend. Pamela, I thought it over. It makes my stomach hurt just thinking about going back to school. I'm taking the summer. So don't register me, okay? I mean it. I'm not coming back until August. I need this break," Hope said firmly.

Surprisingly, Pamela agreed, "Okay honey. I didn't mean to rush you. You relax, okay? Maybe I could figure out a way to come between sessions, for a quick visit. Take care Hope. I miss you."

"I miss you too."

"Do you?" Emerson said, after Hope put the phone down.

"Do I what?"

"Miss her?"

Hope thought a minute. "No. I should, but I don't. I feel an overwhelming sense of relief when I'm not with her."

"This is not good."

"I know."

"Why do you live with someone that makes you so nervous?"

"Because she didn't always make me nervous. She used to make me feel invigorated, excited, like some strange sort of high."

"And now in detox you are seeing the error of your ways," Emerson said, putting the phone back in the mysterious box.

"I thought Berlin said you didn't have a phone," Hope inquired.

"I don't. Let's go have lunch. My treat."

"I'd love to," Hope said, her eyes lighting up.

As they went down the stairs, Emerson said, "I'm awfully proud of you for standing up for yourself."

"Thanks for helping me do it."

"You're not mad then?" Emerson asked tentatively.

"No, I'm not mad."

"Good."

Rachel looked out the café window to see Hope and Emerson jumping in circles in the middle of the park.

"Berlin, what do you suppose they're doing?" Rachel inquired.

Berlin came and stood next to her, "I believe they're called three-sixties. If I didn't know better, I'd say Emerson is teaching Hope how to jump."

"On skates, the trick on the courthouse stairs, oh my god. I'm going to put a quick stop to this," Rachel said.

Berlin caught her arm. "No you're not."

"Why not?"

"Because Emerson is teaching Hope the most important lesson of her life."

"What? How to kill herself?"

"No, how to believe in herself. Emerson won't let her get hurt. She loves her."

"Not that again."

"It's true. You watch them together. They haven't consummated anything yet, but it doesn't mean they're not falling in love."

Rachel watched them for a moment or two. Hope finally did a complete three-sixty, and they both did the high five. Emerson patted her on the back and tousled her hair.

"Damn, that was good. You'll be ready to do it on skates soon," Emerson said, smiling ear to ear.

"When? Let's try it now," Hope said, full of enthusiasm.

"Oh no, not yet. We still need a few more dry runs. Pamela will be furious with me if I send you back in a cast or without your front teeth," Emerson said.

"I don't want to think about going back. I just want to live now without a thought to the future," Hope said.

"All right, let's think about now and something to drink, okay?" Emerson said.

That night Rachel sat across the bed from Hope and listened to her story about how Emerson saved the day. Rachel smiled.

"I'm glad you didn't let her intimidate you. And I'm glad you're staying."

"Rach, I think I misjudged Emerson. She's really a very sweet woman," Hope said.

"She is. Actually, she has grown up quite a bit, and I think the thing with Angel is finally coming to rest. Which is good. It needs to."

"How did Angel treat her? Was she good to Emerson?"

Rachel sat back on her bed and thought a moment. "I'm probably not the best judge of this, but I think she used to fuck with Emerson's head for the fun of it. And she was jealous, violently jealous, of Emerson's talent. Used to sabotage things. Fuck up days when Emerson needed to be working," Rachel said.

"Maybe she'll meet someone nice someday," Hope said, nestling under the covers.

Rachel clicked off the light, thinking, She already has.

Seven

The saloon was quickly filling up with townies and tourists alike. Rachel watched the out of towners take tables and order. She set the timer on her watch. It was an old habit, keeping track of how long it took the tourists to figure out that most of the local color was gay and predominantly lesbian. Dancing usually gave it away, but most times they caught on before the music kicked in. The looks on their surprised faces always gave her a chuckle. For once, straight people were the minority. Rachel liked the feeling. See how you like it, she thought smugly.

The tent dykes had promised Berlin they'd stop by. Rachel accused Berlin of setting them up. Berlin fervently denied it, smiling duplicitously.

Hope was at the bar talking to Berlin and waiting for their drinks.

Rachel sat with Emerson, who was busy rearranging the sundry items on the table into various patterns.

"You like Hope, don't you?" Rachel asked.

Emerson looked up. "What?"

"You heard me. You like her, don't you?"

"Yeah, I like her. She's fun."

"No, Emerson, you know what I mean."

Emerson's blue eyes met Rachel's dark ones.

"No, I don't think I do."

"Like her like a lover."

"She's married. Remember?"

"Not happily."

"You're the one who said we should be friends," Emerson countered.

"I didn't say fall in love."

"I'm no longer capable of that."

"I wouldn't be so sure."

"Rachel, what are you trying to say?" Emerson asked.

"I'm trying to say that you need to be careful for your sake and for hers. Neither one of you is emotionally strong. I just want you to be careful. I don't want either one of you to get hurt. That's all."

"I know. We'll be careful," Emerson said, smiling.

Rachel wasn't so sure. Berlin was right. They looked at each other too long, too intensely, too full of things that shouldn't be.

Hope sat down.

"Rachel, who is that man at the counter with the pictures?"

"That's Clive."

"What's he doing with those photos?" Hope asked.

"Fiddling with the past when he should be living in the present. He drinks and rearranges them. He's convinced if he comes up with the right combination, things will turn out differently," Rachel answered.

Hope furrowed her brow and watched him. He was talking to himself and moving the pictures about.

"What happened to make him like that?" Hope asked.

"Everything bad," Emerson answered.

"His business went bad, his wife left, his dog died, his children won't speak to him, and he's an alcoholic," Rachel said.

"Was he an alcoholic before or after everything fell apart?" Hope asked.

"Does it matter?" Emerson inquired.

"Yes," Hope responded adamantly.

"Why?" Emerson asked.

"Because if he was, then you can blame his decline on drink. But if he became an alcoholic after, you have to blame whimsical fate, which raises the esoteric question of why some people lead charmed lives and others don't," Hope said.

Emerson looked at her appreciatively. "I love your mind."

Hope blushed.

"He took to drink after things went sour. He had bad luck," Rachel said.

"Or maybe he kept making the wrong choices," Emerson said.

"I hope I don't end up like that, making wrong

choices and sitting at some bar endlessly rearranging my life like some bad puzzle, only to discover the pieces never did fit together," Hope said.

"You won't," Emerson said.

"Won't I?" Hope asked.

"No," Emerson said, their eyes meeting.

Watching them, Rachel thought Berlin was right. They were saying things in the unspoken language of lovers. This wasn't supposed to be happening. Rachel had promised Pamela that she would bring Hope back happy and healthy, not in love with someone else. Pamela would hate her until the end of time.

The tent dykes arrived, ordered drinks, and engaged in small talk. Rachel tried her best to be cordial because Hope was shy and Emerson was usually too rude to be counted on for help. Rachel felt the stress of playing the hostess. She silently cursed Berlin.

Emerson surprised her by behaving well; she was almost cordial. She and Amy talked about art school. They'd both been through similar hoops. Hope sat listening until Denise gently touched her arm.

"You probably don't remember me, but I was in one of the classes you were a TA in, the one on Medusa, Muse, and Madonna by Professor Severson," Denise said. "I was at Smith for a year before I went to Berkeley."

Hope groaned.

"What?" Denise asked.

"I hated that class. I hated being a teaching assistant, but Pamela forced me into it."

"I thought you were great. You listened to us and you let us talk about things. In fact, if it hadn't been for your study group, I don't think a lot of us would have got through," Denise said, her eyes sparkling with admiration."

"I thought you looked familiar, but I couldn't place you. I was so nervous all the time. The whole class seemed like one big blur of anxiety," Hope confessed. They were both shocked by her honesty.

"I'm sorry," Hope said.

"Don't be," Denise said, smiling empathetically. "We've all been there. You didn't look nervous."

"I must have put up a good front."

"I know this is kind of a personal question, but you and Professor Severson were lovers, weren't you?"

Hope looked over at Emerson, who was pretending not to listen. "Yes. Were we that obvious?"

"I don't know if I would call it obvious, but you could sense there was a definite chemistry."

They weren't lovers then but had become lovers later. Pamela was Hope's adviser; she pushed her to do things like teach a class. Hope was smart and Pamela saw it. She just needed confidence. Hope agreed to help in the class only because Pamela was teaching it. She had taken several of Pamela's classes because she was completely enamored with the professor. Plus, the classes were packed with other lesbians, none of whom Hope ever had the balls to talk to, but she liked being around them. She cursed being shy, but she couldn't help it.

Her one amazing feat was going by Professor Severson's office with a question she'd spent days devising. They'd talk. Hope did this most of her senior year. She asked Pamela to write her a letter of recommendation for grad school. Pamela saw to it that Hope got in. Working together gave them the perfect excuse to spend time alone. Hope remembered the night they kissed, the same night they made love.

Pamela had her over for dinner saying it was the least she could do to feed a hungry student. Hope couldn't remember what they had for dinner, only that there was a lot of wine. Somewhere in the midst of the talk, Pamela reached over and kissed her.

"I've been wanting to do that for the longest time," Pamela told her.

Hope was frightened, but at the same time she was totally smitten. There was nothing left to do but let herself be seduced. She'd waited, imagined, written the script in her head a thousand times for this moment. She tried to brace herself for the disappointment of dream becoming reality. But Pamela had not crushed her dreams. Instead, she was gentle, not pushy, expectant, or overwhelming. She must have sensed that Hope was fragile.

When it was over, Hope half expected to be another one of Professor Severson's conquests. But the next morning, a vase of white lilies was sitting on her desk, and her fellow graduate students gave her more than a few inquiring looks. She read the card: YOU'RE WONDERFUL. TONIGHT?

Shyly, she went to Pamela's office.

"Hi," Hope said, standing in the doorway.

"Come in," Pamela said, smiling at her.

"Thanks for the flowers," Hope said.

Pamela shut the door behind them. She took Hope in her arms, nestling her face in Hope's soft neck. "I can't stop thinking about you."

And that's how it started. Pamela had finally found her child/lover/protégé wrapped up in a beautiful package of blond innocence. She was ecstatic.

Hope found a woman strong and big enough to make up for all she lacked. She moved in, and Pamela began arranging her life for her.

"She must be quite the girlfriend. I can't even imagine having someone like that around," Denise said.

"Never a dull moment, that's for sure," Hope said, emptying her glass. "Do you like Berkeley?"

"Yes, I like it a lot," Denise said.

"Not quite as stuffy, eh?" Hope said.

"Yeah," Denise said.

"Can I get you another drink?" Emerson asked, picking up her empty glass.

Hope looked up at her. "Trying to get me liquored up, are you?" Hope chided.

"I would never," Emerson said with mock indignation.

"You'll make sure I get home in one piece," Hope flirted back.

"Safe and sound," Emerson said, trotting off to the bar. Hope watched her go, admiring her princely stride. Emerson reminded her of the chevaliers.

"Are you and Pamela still together?" Denise asked.

"In a manner of speaking," Hope said, coming back to meet Denise's gaze. "She's in New York doing those academic things, and I'm taking a breather."

Emerson brought her drink back as well as another for Denise. Both women smiled at her appreciatively.

Denise and Hope talked schools, and Emerson and Amy talked art trends. Charlene, Lily, and Rachel told dyke jokes until they got to laughing so hard that soon everyone was involved. It even drew Berlin, who had a few good mainstays of her own. Lily was absolutely hysterical. She should have been a stand-up comic, not an accounting major.

"An accountant has to have a sense of humor, you know," Lily told Rachel.

Emerson leaned over to whisper in Hope's ear, "Walk in the park?"

Hope looked over and smiled. "Please. I think I've had enough of bar life for one night.

"We're going to go," Emerson told Rachel.

Lily touched Rachel's arm. "Stay for another one?"

"Yeah, Rach, stay. I'll walk Hope home," Emerson said.

They went to the park.

"Oh how nice. I forgot there's a full moon to-night," Hope said, looking up at the sky.

"I wouldn't ask you to go out for any old walk," Emerson said. "I thought we could lie under my favorite tree and take a little moon bath."

"And how does one do that, pray tell?" Hope asked.

"All you have to do is lie there, think good thoughts, and soak up moon rays. It's simple."

"Everything is simple to you," Hope chided.

Emerson smiled. "That's right. I'm done with complex; it takes too much out of you. Simple. Things must be simple."

"Is that why you keep to yourself?" Hope asked, at they sat down beneath a gigantic elm.

"Yes. People are too complicated most of the time."

"And what am I?" Hope asked.

"You're my pretty little friend," Emerson said.

"Emerson, why don't you ever say my name?"

It was quiet for a minute, and then Emerson looked over at her. "Because it's a word I no longer use, am no longer capable of using."

"When will you be able to say it?"

"Probably never."

"That's not very positive."

"So lie back, palms to the sky, and moon bathe. We'll work on positive," Emerson instructed.

"You are a queer woman," Hope said lying back.

They were silent. Hope found it soothing lying beneath the immense star-filled sky, bright with moonlight, the cool earth beneath them, the grass and trees smelling musty.

"Emerson, the statue in the main square is your great-grandfather."

"Yes."

"So why is your first name Emerson when it's really your family name?"

"Because my mother named me after the wishing well near the old house. She said she wished for me and I came, so she named me that."

"That's neat. She must have been an incredible woman."

"I wish I could have known her. But Katherine knew her. If it wasn't for Katherine, I wouldn't know my mother at all."

"Rachel says they were lovers, your mother and Katherine."

"They were. I guess that makes Katherine all the more special to me."

They lay quiet again.

"Tell me about when you first fell in love with Pamela," Emerson said.

"Why?"

"Because I want to know what you are like when you fall in love," Emerson said, leaning up on one elbow. Hope kept looking at the stars.

"I don't really know what I'm like. I think I get kind of scattered, forgetful with the everyday stuff, and hungry."

"Hungry? Why hungry?"

"Because when I'm happy I have a voracious appetite. Everything tastes better, smells better, is better when you're in love," Hope said, rolling over on her side.

"You are confusing infatuation with love," Emerson said wryly.

"Maybe, but does it matter in the end?"

"It does if that's all it ends up being."

"And if it doesn't?"

"Then you have all those rose-colored memories to sustain you through the times when you experience loathing for the one you love," Emerson said.

"Exactly. We need those or no two people on this earth would still be together. Memory and promise are the two things that give us the will to live."

"You think so?"

"Yes, one is the past and the other is the future. The present is the place where both are made, the drawing room of sorts, the place creation takes hold, making the future, holding the past."

"Wow," Emerson said, lying back down. "That's what I like about you. You make me think."

"Yeah, right."

"Why do you do that?"

"Do what?"

"Cut yourself down like that."

"Habit, I guess."

"Well, it's one I'm going to make you break," Emerson said.

Hope didn't tell her it was a habit because she had spent most of her life around people who thought she was an intellectual savage, roaming wild with ideas and thoughts that did nothing but create a web of unanswerable, esoteric questions. But Hope liked the questions, liked pondering impenetrable things. Both her mother and Pamela had tried to curb those tendencies. Hope simply hid them when she finally realized the conspiracy.

"I like when you talk about those things," Emerson said. "They're interesting and not like that everyday stuff that sometimes seems so tedious."

"Hang around long enough and you'd grow to find the esoteric tedious as well," Hope said.

Emerson flicked her hard with her forefinger.

"Ow. Why'd you do that?" Hope asked, rubbing her shoulder.

"I told you I'm going to break you of that habit."

"And what if I like my habit and I don't give it up?"

"It's a bad habit, and you should."

"And if I don't . . ."

Emerson got her flicker finger poised.

Hope grabbed her wrist. Their eyes locked.

Emerson gently loosened Hope's hand, holding it for a moment.

"May I draw your hands tomorrow?"

"Only if you don't flick."

Emerson put her palm to Hope's, comparing the two. Hope watched her. Without letting herself think, Hope closed her fingers around Emerson's. The question lingered in both their eyes. Hope let go, brushed a stray ringlet from Emerson's shoulder, touched her cheek briefly, and said, "You should take me home."

They stopped in front of the house. The living room light was still on.

"Tomorrow?" Emerson asked.

"Yes."

"Emerson."

"Yes?"

"Thank you."

"For what?" Emerson asked, puzzled.

"For the way you make me feel," Hope said, quickly kissing her forehead and running up the stairs to the house.

Emerson stood for a moment like one of her statues. She took off running, ran all the way home past Rachel and Lily standing in front of the café.

"Emerson, what's wrong?" Rachel asked.

"Nothing. Nothing's wrong," Emerson screamed as she flew past.

"Are you sure they're not lovers?" Lily asked.

"I don't know anymore."

"Are you coming by the fair tomorrow?"

"I hadn't planned on it," Rachel said absently.

Lily caught her chin where it had followed Emerson, turning Rachel to face her. "Why don't you?"

"All right," Rachel said.

The next morning Rachel caught her mother alone in the kitchen. Berlin was still upstairs sleeping it off. Hope was out back taking her coffee with the paper. Rachel watched Hope through the window. Sometimes she wondered if Hope really read the paper or if she used it as a shield so she could muse without interruption. Rachel was inclined to think the latter.

"Mom?"

"Yes, dear?" Katherine said, looking up from the pan of scrambled eggs she was making.

"Berlin thinks Hope and Emerson are falling in love. At first I didn't believe her, but after seeing them together last night I think she's right. I'm worried."

"Why are you worried?"

"Because I don't think it's a good idea."

"It's not your place to decide that."

Rachel furrowed her brow, confused. "They're my friends. I don't want them to get hurt."

Katherine took Rachel by the shoulders. "If you love them, you'll let them go."

"What do you mean?"

"Sometimes the greatest gift you can give someone is letting go. I know you still love Emerson and you love Hope, but she's not yours to have."

"She's not Emerson's either."

"But she is. Rachel, you'll find the right one. Those two are the right ones for each other."

"Why is everyone so certain this is right?" Rachel said, pulling away, her face crimson with anger. "This isn't the Delphi Chronicles."

"Rachel, do you remember when Berlin told you about Sarah and me?"

"Yes."

"I loved Sarah. I loved her more than I thought

83

possible, but when I saw that I couldn't give her all the things she needed to be happy, I let her go. When I met Berlin I realized that as much as I loved Sarah, she wasn't the right one for me. Berlin was. Berlin was never second-best. We were each other's right ones. If you and Hope became lovers, it would be because you want to save her from Pamela. Hope and Emerson as lovers would be each saving the other and in the process saving themselves."

"Saving each other from what?"

"From a nasty world full of nasty people."

"What?"

"Neither one of them are rat-race people. You are. You thrive on it. Why do you think Hope doesn't want to be a professor? She doesn't want it because she doesn't like competing and always trying to outdo everyone. Hope is one of those wondering types who wants to be left alone to explore herself. She's not really interested in what's going on out here. She's only interested in the sensations and in cultivating the experiences that produce them. Hope's one great achievement will be herself, and that's all she wants. Emerson can give her the space because she's a lot like her. You can't. She'd only be trading one evil for another."

"So now I'm evil," Rachel said indignantly. "How do you know all this, anyway?"

"The Delphi Chronicles, darling," Katherine answered smugly. Actually, Hope had simply told her one day. If Rachel really listened, Hope would have told her. But Hope and Katherine knew that Rachel, being a doer and not a thinker, would not understand.

"I give!" Rachel said, storming off.

"What's her deal?" Berlin said, walking into the kitchen looking like hell.

"Plagued by the Delphi Chronicles."

Rachel came storming back in. "And just for the record, I am not in love with Hope!'

Hope, hearing her name screamed in the kitchen, came back from her wanderings, set the paper down, and looked inquisitively at Rachel.

"Rach, are you okay?" she asked.

"I'm fine, I'm just fine," Rachel said, walking off.

"Wait," Hope called.

"What?" Rachel said tensely.

"What's wrong?" Hope said, taking Rachel's hand.

Rachel shrugged her shoulders, thinking of what she should say but couldn't. I'm in love with you. You're in love with Emerson. And Pamela is going to ruin my academic career out of retribution for causing the whole sordid mess, which I did not. Instead she said, "Nothing, just mother-daughter shit."

"Come to the fair with Emerson and me?"

"Sure, I promised Lily I would go," Rachel said.

"She's not happy about this thing with Emerson and Hope, is she?" Berlin said, pouring herself a large glass of tomato juice and watching the two of them in the backyard.

"Not in the least."

"I wouldn't have thought Rachel an impediment," Berlin said.

"It's hard when everyone around you is in love and you're not. Besides, I don't think she has quite forgiven Emerson for breaking her heart."

85

"They were too young," Berlin said. "Those ones never last."

"True," Katherine replied, thinking of Sarah.

"Where did we come up with the Delphi Chronicles anyway?" Berlin asked.

"When Rachel was little and we would tell her things, she always wanted to know how we knew. We made up the Delphi Chronicles as the place where all right answers come from, and that satisfied her," Katherine said.

"She was such an inquisitive child," Berlin said, taking two aspirin.

"She still is. Only now the Delphi Chronicles don't fly."

"But we're still right," Berlin said.

"She doesn't think so."

"The young never want to believe the old. Do they think all this living means nothing, that in all we've seen we learned nothing? I have a good mind to swat her butt and tell her to straighten up," Berlin said, sitting down suddenly. "After my head stops hurting."

"Yes, darling," Katherine said, taking Berlin's head in her arms.

Eight

Rachel found Emerson sketching Hope when she arrived at the studio. She promised herself she would behave.

"I'm going to do her hands," Emerson said excitedly. "I mean, look at them. They're exquisite."

"I highly doubt that is the only exquisite part of Hope that inspires you," Rachel said wryly.

Emerson cocked her head and smiled.

Rachel looked at the two of them. Her mother and Berlin were right. She could no longer deny it.

"Pamela's going to kill me," Rachel groaned, putting her head in her hands as she sat on the bed.

Hope sat behind her and rubbed her shoulders. "Will you relax? None of this is your fault."

"I should never have brought you here," Rachel said.

"It was the best thing anyone has ever done for me."

Rachel turned to look at her. "And what about Pamela? How is she going to feel?"

"No matter what happens, Pamela is a survivor of the fiercest order. You forget who we're talking about here," Hope said.

"It's true then," Rachel said, still hoping they'd deny it.

Hope looked over at Emerson. "I want it to be true."

"And what about you?" Rachel asked.

"Ditto," Emerson replied, staring at Hope.

"And we all agree upon what this *it* is," Rachel said.

"Tacitly, yes," Emerson replied.

Hope smiled. Both she and Emerson were on love's autopilot, reckless toward their destination, incapable of stopping. That was the funny thing about love, Hope thought. You forget to be cautious, you forget the pain you once felt, and you remember only what it feels like to look into your lover's eyes and see love reflected back.

"Come on. Let's go meet Lily. We'll have some Indian fry bread and a couple of cold beers, and you'll feel much better," Hope said.

Rachel looked at her queerly. "How come I'm the only one that feels bad here?"

Hope took Rachel's arm and led her to the door. "Because currently the rest of us are behaving amorally."

Emerson tousled Hope's hair and smiled, and the three of them set off toward the hubbub of downtown.

Lily's pleasure at seeing Rachel was obvious. Emerson nudged Hope, who nodded back in agreement. Lily was darling, and if Rachel would stop being angry at the world long enough, she might see it.

"Emerson, how come you don't put your stuff in the art fair?" Lily asked as they stood in front of a stall of bronzes.

"Because Emerson is a snob," Rachel replied.

"I am not!" Emerson said indignantly.

"You are. You don't have your stuff in here because you are high art and not crafty art, fine artist versus craftsperson," Rachel replied.

Emerson scowled at her. "I don't want to talk about it. Besides, my pieces are too big and no one would buy them anyway. I refuse to sit in a stall all day and have people walk by, ogle, and then move on. It's degrading."

Hope looked at Emerson, the sensitive artist, with a new appreciation. She hadn't given much thought to Emerson's work. Emerson the artist hadn't evolved yet. Emerson was her friend, her skating buddy, her protector, and then the other thing, the one she hadn't allowed herself to think of yet, though she felt it moving about, quivering in that half daylight of thought, the shadow land of want.

Wanting was a new experience for Hope. That morning as she sat behind the newspaper, she pondered the concept of desire, discovering that she had never truly experienced it. Her other lovers — there hadn't been many, desired her, hunted her, seduced her. She played captured willingly and sometimes with great design. Her lovers aroused desire in her, but she didn't create it on her own. She took their cues, a well-instructed acolyte but never the high priestess of love.

Pamela had discerned this and brought it to Hope's attention.

"You don't think about me like I think about you. I sit there and think about tracing the outline of your body, about tasting and smelling you. You only think about wanting me when I present it."

Hope did her best not to look guilty, but they both knew it was true. She tried, tried to think about wanting, visualizing Pamela in the throes of passion, but somehow she couldn't quite pull it off. Her fantasies came off as botched scenes in a cheesy romance novel.

But now there was this quivering about of something like want. She found herself thinking about Emerson a lot.

The sensitive artist image was wholly new and afforded an entirely different set of variables to ponder.

Hope was sitting across from Emerson, beneath

an umbrella to keep off the blazing Arizona sun. Summer, it appeared, had officially arrived. Lily and Rachel were discussing some social phenomena both their respective academic interests catered to.

It came out that Lily, although she was getting a degree in accounting, also minored in psychology. The psychological easily meshed with the sociological. Emerson rolled her eyes at both disciplines with equal disgust. For Emerson there was nothing but art. Rachel and Lily jabbered back and forth while Emerson made it apparent she wasn't interested and Hope pretended she was listening, a practice she was well versed in.

And it was at this particular moment that Hope discovered she was falling in love. She hadn't been certain what exactly she was admitting to when Rachel asked, only that she was slowly divesting herself of Pamela. Whether or not she was taking up with Emerson hadn't quite dawned on her. That she was letting go of Pamela was certain. She had been thinking about it for weeks, ever since the phone call. It wasn't something she could discuss with Rachel. She hadn't quite ascertained why. Rachel's anger and frustration didn't make sense, since Rachel didn't like Pamela.

Katherine proved a better confidante. Hope cornered her one morning when Rachel was at work.

"Can I talk to you for a moment?" Hope asked.

"Why sure, darling. Coffee?"

"Please."

"Always best to discuss things over coffee, learned that from my mother, gives you something to do in a tense moment," Katherine replied, thinking of her mother pouring them both coffee, wiping her hands on her floral apron, and taking a seat with extreme solemnity. Talk over coffee was important. Women bonded that way, reaching across kitchen tables to support one another. Kitchens would always be magical places for Katherine. It concerned her that her own daughter didn't have this affinity, making her wonder if she'd raised some sort of feminine monster.

"What is it, darling?" Katherine asked, sensing it must be something Rachel wasn't capable of discussing. And she wondered why Hope wasn't in love with her. The Rachels and Pamelas of the world were Hope's nemeses.

"I think I'm falling out of love. Actually, I'm beginning to wonder if I was ever truly in love or whether I was just in love with the idea of having someone love me. I'm sorry . . ." Hope faltered. "I'm not really making any sense. What I mean is, I don't want to be with Pamela anymore," she blurted.

"You're falling out of love with the woman you thought you were in love with. It was perfectly understandable the first time."

"And I know that people are going to think that it's Emerson's fault, but it's not. She's simply made me think perhaps there is something better, some better way to be. I mean that for both Pamela and me. We were never well suited for each other. Maybe she can find someone more aggressive, more career oriented, you know, someone more like her. I think sometimes I'm more of an irritation than I'm worth."

"And maybe you can find someone more suited to you."

"Well, yes," Hope said, meeting Katherine's gaze.

"But you're worried about what people will think and what Pamela is going to do when she finds out."

"Exactly. It's going to be rather awkward. And I'm not very good at breaking things off."

"How did you break it off before?"

"There's never been anything this serious before. I had dates or casual relationships — dinner, bed at your place or mine. And then I guess it mostly amounted to not returning phone calls."

"Obviously that isn't going to work this time. Pamela doesn't seem like the type to just say okay, honey, it's been nice knowing you, we had some good times didn't we, knock you on the shoulder, and walk out of your life, now is she?"

Hope sat for a moment, envisioning the whole thing. What would she say? Pamela, I'm really sorry, but I don't think I love you anymore. You can't just say that. What was she going to do? This was the first time Hope had actually thought of what good-byes would entail.

"Hope," Katherine said, bringing her back from the fringes of this new and very present nightmare. "You haven't taken up with Emerson, have you?"

"What? No. I'm not even sure we're moving in that direction."

"Well, maybe you should break it off with Pamela first. It might make it a tad neater in the end."

"I wish. But what am I supposed to say? Listen, Emerson, just in case you're entertaining any thoughts of seducing me, perhaps we'd better wait until I'm a free woman."

"I know that might seem awkward, but you know when that moment arrives you could try to forestall it," Katherine advised.

"Until when, though? I can't call Pamela and tell her I don't want to come back just yet. She'll want to know why. And I really do like Emerson. I'm so confused. Katherine, I really don't know what to do," Hope said, her shoulders drooping with the weight of it all.

"We'll figure out something, honey," Katherine assured her.

Now, sitting at the table watching Emerson gently harassing Rachel and winking at her, Hope knew. This was a moment she knew she would never forget, the way the sun shone on Emerson's hair, the little streaks of red, the way her hair fell about her face, the small grimace she made when something disagreeable came up. Hope memorized it all. It was a strange moment when the present was sent dashing into the future and coming back with its knowledge like a dog sent fetching. In years to come, she would look back on this moment and remember it, the day, the minute, the second, she fell in love, and they would roll about in bed together remembering it. Hope suddenly wondered when Emerson's moment would come.

Emerson touched Hope's hand. "What are you thinking?"

Hope snapped back to the present. "It's something I'll have to tell you later, much later," she replied, smiling.

Emerson crinkled her brow, puzzled. "Okay."

Rachel looked over at them and didn't know whether to laugh or cry over the whole thing. It wasn't wasted on Lily. Later, when the two of them were alone, she called Rachel on it.

"So let me guess. You've got a thing for one of them. I haven't quite figured out which one, but something's got to give. Confess, it will make you feel better," Lily said.

Rachel gave a heavy sigh. "Let's go get a bite to eat, and I'll try to explain."

Over Swiss cheese, avocado, and sprout sandwiches, Rachel confessed.

"It's a question of love, but who loves whom and who gets whom? Personally, I think you should let those two go and take up with me. I'm single, I'm amusing, and I promise not to break your heart," Lily said, tilting her head, curving her lip, and trying her best to look appetizing.

"Don't tempt me," Rachel said, smiling. If she could get over losing her two best friends to each other, she might give it, go.

As they turned to leave, Lily grabbed her arm. "I'm a patient woman, Rachel, and I'm willing to wait. I meant what I said."

"I know," Rachel said, looking deep into Lily's eyes and reading truth there. "I'll work on it, okay?"

"I'm going to hold you to that," Lily said. "I should warn you, I'm famous for my diligence."

That night Rachel went to sleep thinking of things other than Hope and Emerson. And when she didn't wake up crabby, her mother took notice.

Nine

"Emerson, I don't think I'm grasping the concept here," Hope said, as Emerson poured another handful of sunflower seeds into the palm of her hand.

"If you're going to be a blader, you've got to master seeds. Now concentrate. Think about your tongue and what it's doing," Emerson explained.

"If I master seeds, do I get to do the jump?" Hope asked.

"Yes," Emerson replied, giving Hope a rather forceful tap on the head. "Ski jump."

Hope looked shocked and then promptly choked on her mouthful of seeds. She turned from pink to blue in a matter of seconds.

Emerson got behind her and started to squeeze, performing the necessary first aid to assist a choking victim.

"No, no. I'm fine. Please don't squeeze me like that; you're hurting my ribs," Hope said.

"I'm sorry, I'm so sorry. I didn't mean to hurt you," Emerson said, holding her more gently. She was about to let go when Hope took her hand.

"No, stay for a moment."

Emerson lay against Hope's back. "I love the way you smell."

"Like what?"

"Like you. I'm taking liberties, you know."

"I know, and I like them."

"Are you sure?"

"Yes, I'm sure. Now when do I get to jump?" Hope asked, turning around to face Emerson.

"Well, since you survived the choking part of seeds, I guess now is as good a time as any," Emerson said, helping her up.

They started off toward the courthouse. The townspeople were none too happy about having two bladers, one as reckless as the other. Rachel, her mother, and Berlin were sitting outside the café when they both came dashing by at lightning speed.

"Hope's skating really has improved, don't you think?" Berlin asked.

"Oh my god, this has really gone too far. Now we have two of them," Rachel said.

"Is this fuddy-duddy stage of yours just a passing

thing or are we going to have to call in an exorcist? I don't want a child of mine to grow up stodgy," Berlin said.

"But I'm not your child, really," Rachel said plainly.

"Ah, but you are, my dear," Berlin said.

"Not birth child."

"Yes, dear, birth child, in the womb nine months, and believe me it wasn't fun. But I love you just the same. I've forgiven you for the ugly things you used to do to me as an embryo. Time is a great healer," Berlin replied, putting on her best prophetic sage look.

"I thought I was adopted," Rachel said, looking at Katherine.

"Why would you think that?" Berlin asked, looking perturbed.

"Because both my parents are lesbians," Rachel ventured.

"So what does that have to do with anything?" Berlin said.

"Don't you think we would have told you by now if you had been adopted?" Katherine asked.

"Well, I just figured I was. You two are my parents. I didn't need to look any further. One of those unsaid things."

"Berlin, I thought you told her," Katherine said.

"I thought you told her," Berlin replied.

"Shit, it would have been nice if someone had told me."

"You were my Christmas present," Katherine said, squeezing Berlin's hand.

"So how'd you manage it?" Rachel asked.

"The usual way," Berlin snapped.

"Who was he?"

"A very nice man. Unfortunately, he is now a dead man. He was a rather reckless sort, died in a car wreck. His name was Clifford, and he was a friend of ours in Britain. That's why I am appalled at your present stodginess, with such flamboyant genes you really shouldn't be so conservative. Now look at Hope. That's nerve," Berlin said, as Hope followed Emerson off the retaining wall of the courthouse doing a perfect three-sixty and landing beautifully.

"Oh my god!" Rachel said, getting up. "I'm going to kill both of them."

"I don't really think that's fair considering they just survived a rather impressive piece of skating. Besides, look at them. Aren't they cute together?" Berlin said. "Kind of makes my heart go pitter-patter," she said, wiping a tear with the corner of her shirt.

Rachel watched them. Emerson had picked Hope up and swung her around. They were both ecstatic at the success and bumping helmets like little frat boys.

"Yeah, we'll all be wiping up tears when Pamela finds out," Rachel said, walking off toward the art fair.

"That was great!" Emerson said, putting Hope down.

Flushed with excitement, Hope said, "Really?"

"Really," Emerson replied, filled with admiration. "You know, I've never had a skating buddy before. This is kind of nice."

"Kind of nice?" Hope said, pinching her.

"Ouch. That hurt," Emerson said, rubbing her arm.

"You deserved it," Hope said, smiling and skating off.

Emerson came up quickly behind her, tackling her onto the grass.

That's how Rachel found them, wrestling around on the grass, laughing.

She looked like the disapproving mother until Emerson grabbed her by the ankles and pulled her down. They both tickled her until she too was laughing.

"That'll teach you to be so uptight," Emerson said.

When they composed themselves, Rachel said, "Lily wants us to come for drinks tonight at the saloon."

"Are we double-dating now?" Emerson said slyly.

"I don't know. Are we?" Rachel retorted.

"We can't. She's married," Emerson replied.

"Am I?" Hope said.

"Are you?" Emerson said.

"Do I have to be?"

"No, not if you don't want to," Emerson said.

"Well, then, I'm not," Hope replied.

"Someone really ought to let your wife know," Rachel said.

"Do we have to? Maybe she could figure it out on her own," Hope said.

"She won't. You're going to have to do the ugly deed," Rachel said.

"Someday, but not today. Today let's have fun. The saloon?" Hope said.

"Yes," Rachel said.

Lily and Rachel stood at the jukebox, putting an endless supply of quarters into it.

"It's scary. We have the same taste in music," Rachel said, as they both chose the same song for the third time in a row.

"Why is it scary?" Lily asked, cocking her head to one side.

"I don't know. That we have so much in common. I wouldn't have figured."

"Let me guess. This is a new sensation for you," Lily said, sticking another quarter in the slot.

"Well, yeah," Rachel admitted.

"Don't tell me you're one of those hopeless souls who always choose the wrong women," Lily said, anticipating Rachel's answer.

Rachel looked away.

"Why? Why do you do that to yourself? Why put your energy into something you know is going to fail?"

"You're analyzing me again," Rachel countered.

"Someone ought to," Lily said.

Rachel was taken aback. "Are you always this forward?"

"Only with people I like. Now tell me why you think you do it."

There was a commotion at the bar. Hope had given Emerson a payback, the ski-jump trick.

"What'd you do that for?" Emerson said, rubbing her forehead.

"I don't know. I just felt like it," Hope said, smiling.

"Well, I'm still bigger than you," Emerson said, plucking Hope off her barstool and twirling her around.

"Emerson! Put me down," Hope demanded.

"Apologize," Emerson said, whirling her around another time.

"All right, already. I'm sorry."

"That's better," Emerson said, putting her down.

The jukebox kicked in.

"Come dance with me," Emerson said, suddenly pulling Hope toward the bar's tiny dance floor. Emerson gently took Hope in her arms, and together their bodies swayed.

Rachel and Lily stood watching.

Rachel met Lily's inquiring gaze. "I think I fall in love with the wrong people because I want it to fail. I'm afraid of falling in love because I don't want to get hurt again," Rachel gushed, feeling her face flush. "There. I said it."

"Don't you feel better?" Lily asked.

"No, I'm embarrassed that I told someone I hardly know something I can't make myself confide to my best friend."

"That's because you're in love with your best friend. Don't worry. I plan on being more than a stranger. Let me buy you a drink, and I'll confess some deep dark secret and we'll be even."

"Okay," Rachel said, thinking, And when you walk out of my life it will hurt just like all the others. It's a question of love, and the answer is always no.

Emerson and Hope stayed dancing, lovers on the verge of becoming lovers getting to know each other's bodies. Later they sat in the park, a blanket wrapped around them, Emerson sitting behind Hope, keeping her warm, watching the stars.

"Emerson?"

"Yes," Emerson murmured, her face nestled in Hope's hair.

"This has been the best summer I've ever had. Thank you."

"You want to know a secret?"

"What?"

"I didn't think I could ever feel this way."

"What way is that?"

"I can't tell you now. I'll have to tell you later, much later."

Hope turned to look at her and smiled. She squeezed her hand.

"I should take you home. I think dawn is catching up with us," Emerson said.

"Do we have to?"

"We can't stay here all night," Emerson said.

"Can't we?" Hope said, pulling her down.

Emerson wrapped her arms around Hope, their faces touching. "I guess we could."

"Hmm," Hope said, closing her eyes and pulling Emerson in closer.

Rachel came downstairs to find her mother and Berlin perusing the paper. The house was getting the *New York Times* courtesy of Hope.

"We really ought to go. We haven't traveled in eons," Berlin said.

"Go where?" Rachel asked.

"Why Europe, darling," Katherine said. "Look how cheap the airfare is now."

"I had no idea," Berlin said.

"Don't be blowing my trust fund," Rachel said.

"I would never, darling," Berlin said, kissing her forehead.

"Where's Hope?" Rachel asked, suddenly realizing she was nowhere in sight.

Katherine and Berlin both looked at each other guiltily.

Rachel caught it immediately. "She didn't come home."

"Now we don't know that for certain. Maybe she got up early. I'm sure she'll show up sooner or later," Katherine said, trying to defuse a tense situation.

"Yeah, I'm sure she will. Well, I'm off to the café, I'm meeting Lily for breakfast," Rachel said.

Berlin and Katherine made faces at each other, like that was different.

"Lily?" Berlin said.

"Maybe we'll be having a double wedding by the end of summer," Katherine said.

Rachel and Lily had eaten, and Lily left for another day of rearranging tents for the next scheduled fair in two weeks. This was the gay and lesbian fair, the one everyone in town was anticipating. It would be a nonstop party weekend because the fair coincided with the town's pride festival. The town would be packed with tourists. Business would be booming.

Berlin was fumbling her way through her version

of numerology, looking for her latest lottery numbers. The lottery was one form, the only form, of gambling that Berlin was not entirely successful at, but she was working on it. She was gazing out the window when she noticed the lump of blanket in the middle of the park, a shock of blond hair next to a curly mess of brown.

"Rachel, I believe I've found our delinquents," Berlin said, pointing in the direction of the park.

Rachel, Katherine, and Berlin stood at the window. It was definitely Hope and Emerson.

"Take them some coffee and breakfast, will you, Rach? It'll be fun for them to have a picnic breakfast in the park. Go on, get moving. We wouldn't want them charged with vagrancy, would we?" Berlin said, nudging Rachel.

Hope smelled coffee. She thought she was hallucinating until she opened her eyes to find Rachel holding breakfast.

"I'm famished," Hope said, sitting up.

Emerson followed, smiling big at Rachel. "Me too. What a gal, Rachel."

"It was actually Berlin's idea," Rachel admitted.

They spread out the blanket and sat down to breakfast.

"Have you ever spent the night in a park before?" Rachel asked Hope.

"No, can't say that I have."

"Emerson, of course, has. She used to sleep in the park all the time until Lutz threatened police action if she didn't stop," Rachel said.

"And we all know how claustrophobic I am," Emerson replied, shoveling in the last of her hash browns.

"So what's up?" Rachel finally asked.

"Nothing," Hope replied. "Well, something, but not what you're thinking, not yet at least, not in a park."

"I definitely draw the line at parks," Emerson said, thinking, No, they hadn't made love. But she'd held the woman she loved in her arms all night. She'd listened to her stir, watched her sleep, held her so close they could feel each other breathe. Emerson couldn't remember when she had ever been this happy. And for once she wasn't thinking about getting hurt. Her one obstacle to happiness lay in another woman's hands. A woman she'd never met, but one she had the good sense to be afraid of.

Ten

"I figured out a way to get you to pose for me," Emerson said.

"I highly doubt that," Hope replied, looking out the window at the tent crews below. It seemed that the whole town was being rearranged. She could see Lily organizing the affair: attractive and brainy. Rachel could be extremely fortunate if she'd let herself.

Hope had never quite figured out Rachel's aversion to relationships. Did it all stem from the thing with Emerson? My god, they were sixteen, and it was puppy love. You can't let a thing like that scar your entire life. What was Rachel afraid of? Hope wondered.

"Emerson, why do you suppose Rachel hasn't found herself a mate?"

"Because she's picky, uptight, and self-centered," Emerson offered.

"Aren't we all, whether we admit it or not. Lily seems crazy about her, and Rachel is nothing but noncommittal. Certainly Rachel has a sex drive. What's wrong with a little summer love?"

"Rachel has a sex drive all right."

"And you would know, you little seducer," Hope chided.

"If I'm such a seducer, how come I haven't got to you?" Emerson said.

"You're waiting until my divorce is final," Hope ventured.

"Are we more than summer love?" Emerson asked, looking up from her work.

Hope stood quiet for a moment and then came across the room. She held Emerson's head against her stomach. "Yes."

"I'm scared," Emerson said, as she wrapped her arms around Hope's waist.

"Me too," Hope said.

"Is that why we're dawdling?" Emerson asked.

Hope leaned down to met Emerson's gaze. "It'll happen when it's supposed to happen." And then she kissed her. Perhaps that would have been the moment had Rachel not come up the stairs.

She saw their flushed faces and knew she was interrupting.

"I just came by to see if you two wanted to come to lunch. Berlin is attempting salmon mousse."

"Actually," Emerson said, as she went to the fridge and pulled out a picnic basket, "I was going to go picnicking with my little friend, if she would so kindly oblige me. But I suppose we could go another day."

"No, you go. Berlin will save you some. Come for dinner then?" Rachel said.

"Yes," Emerson said.

"You two have fun," Rachel said, making for the door.

"Rachel, why don't you come with us?" Emerson asked.

"No, you go. It's all right, Emerson, really. We're all big girls now, and we've been punished long enough."

"She's right, you know," Hope said.

"I know," Emerson said, taking Hope's hand.

"So where are we going and how are we getting there?" Hope asked as they clunked down the stairs, their footsteps echoing against the empty brick walls.

"In my car," Emerson replied.

"I didn't know you have a car," Hope said.

"I'm sure there's lots of things you don't know about me," Emerson said coyly.

"Are there some crucial things you should tell me?"

"Madness runs in my family," Emerson teased.

"Well, we'd better not have any children then," Hope replied.

Emerson stopped and put the picnic basket down. Hope looked on, puzzled.

"Hold me," Emerson said.

Hope took her in her arms. "What's wrong?"

"This is too good. You're too good," Emerson replied.

Hope stroked her cheek, kissed her eyes. "I won't hurt you."

"I know," Emerson said. "Now kiss me again."

And Hope did.

Emerson opened the freight door on the first floor to reveal an MG.

"It's cute," Hope said.

"It's supposed to be cherry red, see," Emerson said, licking her finger and sticking it to the faded hood.

"Is this like the elevator?" Hope asked.

"Yeah, my father gave it to me for a graduation present. After he died and Angel left, I guess I just stopped caring about things."

"Maybe someday you'll want to get them fixed," Hope offered.

"Perhaps I could be enticed," Emerson said, throwing the picnic basket in the back.

"Where are we going?" Hope asked, as she settled in.

"First we have to run a little errand. If that's all right?"

"Sure."

The little errand was more than a little errand, Hope thought as they stood on the hillside that overlooked the convent.

"Angel?" Hope asked.

"Yes," Emerson replied.

"Saying good-bye?"

"Yes."

Hope took her hand.

"Are you okay?" Hope asked.

"Now I am. Thank you for coming with me. I couldn't do it by myself."

"Have you tried before?"

"Yes, but I never had a strong enough reason to truly give up the obsession," Emerson said as they started back toward the car.

"You know, it's funny that we always suffer more for the one that walks away than for the one we leave. I wonder why that is," Hope said.

"Because we didn't choose it."

"And being emotional power-freaks, that bothers us," Hope said.

"That's my guess," Emerson said.

"So where's the picnic?"

"You'll see."

"These are really good," Hope said, biting into her Havarti-and-cucumber sandwich. "Who catered the picnic?"

"I did," Emerson said.

"I didn't think you did things like cook."

"Why would you think that?"

"You never have anything but soda in your fridge."

"It's the living alone thing. Eating by yourself is depressing."

"Can't say it's my favorite thing either," Hope said, thinking about the times she had sat alone at the table, waiting for Pamela and not eating because it was depressing. You shouldn't have to be in love and alone so much. Is that what she would tell Pamela when the time came? She hadn't got that far.

"Emerson, there is something I should tell you."

"What? Another deep, dark secret?"

"No, just a character trait. I'm a horrible procrastinator."

Emerson laughed. "What a bad thing. I don't know if I can live with that."

"I'm serious."

"I know you are. What do you think I am? We'll procrastinate together. Procrastinators should stick together, but somehow we always end up with organizational geniuses. Makes for difficult going."

"I know, but I don't want you to get any nasty surprises. Right now you're under the spell of erotic madness. Lovers are always perfect then."

"It's only later that you find out what a lemon you married."

"Yes, and then everyone is disappointed and confused."

"Is that what happened with Pamela?" Emerson asked as she got out her sketch pad.

"I was the disappointment."

"You didn't live up to her expectations?"

"I think she wanted an academic go-getter, and instead she got me."

"And what are you?" Emerson asked, sketching the outline of Hope's neck. It was a beautiful neck.

"A procrastinating girlfriend who looks good in a dinner jacket and relieves sexual urges in a satisfactory manner."

"What?"

"That's how Pamela describes me."

Emerson's face flushed with anger. "I care about you. I want to be with you, and I promise you'll be more than that to me. I know you're scared and I know it's not going to be fun telling her, but you can't let me go now. I'll be forced to kidnap you if you do."

"I'm not letting go. I just don't want to disappoint you."

Emerson took her in her arms. "You inspire me. Of course, if you'd let me sculpt you . . ."

"Emerson, I don't know."

"I have an idea. See the lake? Let's go swimming."

"Right now?"

"Yes."

"I don't have a suit."

"Exactly," Emerson said, pulling her toward the lake.

"I don't know. I've never done this before."

"You've never skinny-dipped before?"

"Well, no."

"It's high time then," Emerson said, quickly removing her clothes.

"Won't someone see us?"

"No. No one ever comes here."

Emerson stood there naked. Hope swallowed hard. She felt desire. And it was new. She did not remember ever having felt this. Strange for a woman of twenty-six. She thought herself incapable. It was nice discovering the contradiction.

Hope ran her finger along Emerson's collarbone. "You're lovely."

"I'm not supposed to be lovely. You're supposed to look at me so I can look at you, and then I can sculpt you," Emerson said, grabbing Hope's shirt. "Come on, off with it."

Hope obliged. "Sometimes I can't believe the things you get me to do," she said, removing her last articles of clothing.

"Exactly what I expected, " Emerson said, spying her body, looking at its artistic qualities. "You'll be perfect."

"Somehow, I didn't think the first time you looked at my body it would be for its artistic merit."

Emerson smiled and led her to the water. "I'm sure with time I'll discover its other attributes."

They immersed themselves.

"I can't believe you've never been skinny-dipping. Isn't it nice?"

"You were never raised in an uptight Boston family. And yes, this is nice, very nice. But I could think of something that would make it even nicer," Hope said, moving toward Emerson.

Emerson's eyes got big.

"What's wrong?"

"Shh, it's the penguins," Emerson said, pulling Hope to one side of the pond.

"The what?"

"The nuns," Emerson whispered.

"I thought you said no one came here."

"They don't. It's convent grounds."

"Shit, Emerson, you should have told me."

"This is not the time for a discussion. Maybe they didn't see us," Emerson said.

"I don't think your wish is going to come true,"

Hope said as the head nun in the pack of nuns came straight toward them.

"Young ladies, just what do you think you're doing?" the nun asked.

"Swimming," Emerson replied.

"Well, get out right now. These are holy grounds, not the state park."

"I have a better idea. You leave and then we'll get out," Emerson suggested.

"I mean now," the nun replied.

"If you insist," Emerson said.

"Emerson, no," Hope pleaded.

"I've got to do as the good sister says," Emerson responded. She whispered to Hope, "They'll have us arrested, so when we get out grab your clothes and run."

"I'm not running naked in front of a bunch of nuns."

"Do you want to go to jail?"

"No."

"Then run."

They looked like twin Athenas emerging from the pond. Some of the nuns screeched; others stood gazing. The nun in charge got a red face and started to bellow something, but Hope and Emerson were gone. They stopped running when they got over the hill. Emerson fell down laughing. Hope was attempting to sort out her clothing.

"I can't believe this is happening," Hope said.

"I'll bet you've never done that before either," Emerson said.

"Why do I have this sneaking suspicion that if I continue to associate with you stuff like this is going to happen frequently?"

"Never a dull moment. You'll laugh about it when you're old," Emerson said.

"I don't know about that. Naked in front of a bunch of nuns. I can't believe it."

"We probably made their day. They're all little dykes at heart."

"Emerson, that's not nice."

"They've never been nice to me. I'm the one who got carted off, remember? I didn't see any sisterly love then. You're not mad at me, are you?" Emerson asked, suddenly concerned that Hope was not going to forgive her.

Hope smiled. "No, I'm not mad. But next time tell me we're going skinny-dipping on sacred ground. Angel wasn't in that pack of nuns, was she?"

"No, too bad. I could have introduced you."

"Oh yeah."

"You don't have any religious aspirations do you?"

"No, silly."

When they got back to the car, Emerson said, "What do you want to do now?"

"Let's go shopping," Hope said.

"For what?"

"Clothes for you."

"What for?"

"I promised Rachel if I ever got you near Grover's Corner that I'd take you shopping."

"Why? I have clothes."

"No, you have the same three T-shirts."

"I have more than three."

"Metaphorically speaking. Come on, it'll do you

good. Humor me," Hope said, pulling Emerson close and kissing her ardently. "Do you ever get the feeling that every time we're about to make love someone interrupts us?"

"Maybe Pamela is an omniscient wife," Emerson said, kissing Hope's neck.

"Does that bother you?"

"Not if it doesn't bother you," Emerson replied, taking Hope's rear in both hands and pulling her close. "Have I ever told you what a nice tush you have?"

Hope smiled. "No, I don't believe you have. Now shopping?"

"All right."

Emerson stood in shops while Hope picked out clothing. Hope found it enjoyable watching Emerson model each new outfit.

"You are a most attractive woman," Hope said, decidedly pleased.

Emerson smiled and went back into the dressing room to try on yet another outfit. Hope sprawled out on the old settee that the eclectic shop provided for its patrons and waited. She pondered the sensation of loving and being loved. Of desiring and being desired. Each time Emerson emerged from the changing booth and looked to her for approval, Hope felt excitement.

Suddenly she understood the feeling other women described when they saw the one they love walk into the room. She had often wondered about this sensation because she never felt it. She tried to but realized it wasn't a sensation she could conjure up by sheer force of will. Hope decided she was incapable of romantic love with all its trappings. Was this something else she would tell Pamela? She tossed the thought aside like a broken toy when Emerson walked in the room.

When they were finished shopping they packed the back of the MG with shopping bags and went out for dinner. On the way home, Emerson wrapped Hope up in a blanket. Hope nestled up to her, closed her eyes, and fell asleep, looking like a child who had a big day.

Emerson looked down at her, brushed Hope's hair from her eyes, and felt love.

Berlin howled when they told her the story. Hope was having a salmon mousse sandwich. A midnight snack.

"I can't believe you're still hungry after the dinner we had," Emerson said, as Hope stuck her head in the refrigerator looking for something to eat.

Berlin was the only one up when they got home. She'd been out playing poker and was doing her bookkeeping when they got in.

"I can't help it. I'm still hungry," Hope replied.

"Is this a sign of a voracious appetite?" Emerson asked, remembering what Hope had said about being in love making her hungry.

"Looks like it," Hope said.

"Here, have another helping," Emerson said, handing her the plate of salmon mousse.

Berlin peeked around the corner as they said their good-byes. Katherine would admonish her for it in the morning, but she had to know.

"Tomorrow?" Emerson asked, holding Hope in her arms.

"Tomorrow what?" Hope teased.

"You know. You'll pose for me. Please."

"All right. I'll bring you breakfast."

"You're going to make us both fat," Emerson said.

Berlin watched them kiss and then went upstairs, the proud winner of a bet and much knowledge.

Eleven

Emerson listened to Hope's soft sneakers padding up the stairs. She could feel her heart racing. She'd spent most of the night thinking about Hope, allowing herself to dream of what life might be like, which was something she hadn't done in so long that she marveled at her ability to still do it. She could dream again. Emerson lay awake, thinking of how it would feel to touch Hope, to taste her, to feel her smooth skin against her own. She could barely breathe with the anticipation of it all.

But she wanted more than to make love. Emerson

wanted to make Hope her wife. Not like Angel, a chaotic, selfish, frustrated wife, but a lover to share everything with, a lover to grow old and wrinkled with. Emerson furrowed her brow and said a small, silent prayer. For the years of waiting, she had found her one true love.

When Hope's flashing blue eyes and scattered blond hair popped around the corner, Emerson took it as divine intervention.

"Hi," Hope said, suddenly shy, for she too had spent much time thinking about Emerson.

"Good morning. How are you?"

"I'm fine, very fine. Thinking about you constantly. Come here," Hope said, pulling her close.

"I've got everything ready," Emerson said.

"For what?"

"For you to pose. You promised," Emerson said, grabbing Hope's shirt.

"Oh god, not this again. I've never spent so much time naked without the benefit of being seduced in my entire life," Hope said, pulling off her T-shirt.

"We'll get to that," Emerson said, bringing Hope over to a sheet-draped settee. "Right here, like this — arm here, leg there — perfect."

Emerson began to sketch. Hope watched her for a while and then closed her eyes, listening to the early morning noises of the town below. The daydream of making love to Emerson played itself again in Hope's mind. She could hear the lazy buzz of the overhead fan and the scratching of Emerson's charcoal against paper. The scratching stopped. Hope opened her eyes to find Emerson kneeling next to her, looking intently into her eyes.

"Hope, I love you."

Hope kissed her. Emerson kissed her neck, her breasts, her stomach. Slowly Emerson parted Hope's legs. For half a second Hope thought herself lost in the daydream again until she felt those things that only reality brings.

Emerson put her strong, agile fingers inside. Hope closed her eyes and gripped the pillow behind her. They both waited for the oncoming quiver. Hope let go with the abandon of having wanted this for weeks, of needing to feel alive and filled with desire. They barely got Emerson's clothes off before Hope pulled Emerson on top and gently made her cry out with the sheer pleasure of being in love and being touched again.

Hope lay across Emerson's chest. "I'll bet you do this with all your models."

Emerson kissed her forehead. "No, only you. I meant what I said. I love you."

Hope leaned up on one elbow. "I know you do. I never doubted it for a minute. And you want to know a secret?" Hope asked, climbing on top of Emerson and guiding her hand down below. Hope felt her inside and arched her neck like a satisfied feline.

"What's the secret?" Emerson prodded.

Hope opened her eyes. "I love you too, more and bigger than I ever thought myself capable of."

And then they were lost in the land of new lovers, discovering the beauty of each other's bodies until it was late afternoon and they lay sleeping.

That was how Rachel found them, wrapped up and sleeping in one another's arms. She stood for a moment watching them, feeling sad and happy rolled into one confused sensation. She tiptoed back down the stairs.

When she got home, she laid a crisp twenty-dollar bill down in front of Berlin and walked off without saying a word.

"Guess what happened?" Berlin said, snapping the twenty between her fingers.

Katherine smiled. "We were right."

"Damn, if only we could be so prescient about the lottery numbers," Berlin said.

"And just what would you do with all that money?"

"I'd buy the town."

"Berlin, no one else may know it, but I know who owns most of the land in this town. You aren't fooling me with that Dyke Astronomy, Inc. You may have everyone else convinced it's some outfit from California, but I know better."

"Shh, someone might hear you."

"What are you going to do with it?"

"We're going to retire on it. Land is a good investment."

"My god, you are a financial genius. So what would you really do with the lottery money?"

"I'd buy Rachel a new attitude."

Katherine rubbed Berlin's shoulders. "She sees everyone around her in love and she's not. It's a hard thing."

"She won't let herself be in love. What about Lily? Smart, attractive, tits to die for, and the nicest little tush in town, and does she have a thing for Rachel? Yes. Only Rachel's busy being a contorted asshole and can't see five feet in front of her face.

Lily's going to have to jump her bones in order to make an impression."

"If it's meant to be, it'll happen. Now come to bed."

"You have a pretty nice tush yourself," Berlin said, squeezing it.

"Maybe you could jump my bones then," Katherine said, racing her way up the stairs with Berlin hot in pursuit.

Rachel lay in bed listening to them. She got up and quietly slipped out of the house.

She found Lily outside the courthouse having beers with the rest of the tent crew.

"What a nice surprise," Lily said, pulling up a chair for Rachel.

"I need to talk to you."

"We can go to my room. Come on," Lily said, grabbing a couple of beers from the ice chest and bidding her companions good night.

Lily had no sooner shut the door than Rachel pinned her against it and kissed her.

"That was nice," Lily said.

"Take me to bed," Rachel commanded.

"Excuse me?"

"You heard me."

"Are you sure?"

Rachel kissed her and moved her toward the bed. "Yes, I'm sure."

As Rachel was kissing her neck and beginning to unbutton her shirt, Lily asked, "What, may I ask, brought this on? You seemed rather leery about dating, and now —"

"And now I'd really like to make love to you," Rachel said, taking Lily's breast and kissing it gently.

"But," Lily began. Rachel kissed her. Lily gave herself up for lost, pulled off Rachel's shirt, and allowed Rachel to lift her up and let her tongue take what it wanted. Lily leaned her face against the wall and turned her harping doubts down low so she couldn't hear them. All she heard now was her own rapid breathing and Rachel's low moans. She slid down Rachel's chest and reached for her. Rachel opened her eyes and watched Lily take her until she writhed with delight, closed her eyes, and held her lover tight.

Tired, sweaty, and happy, they lay in each other's arms.

"Now, you were saying?" Rachel asked.

"I don't remember now," Lily said, snuggling up closer.

"I have to pee," Rachel said getting up.

Lily lay back, listening. If she thought she was falling in love before, she knew it now. I want to listen to you pee for the rest of my life, she thought to herself. Unfortunately, this was probably a passing fancy, a late-night whim, on Rachel's part. And she had succumbed. Now it would be harder and hurt more when they said good-bye.

Rachel came back. Lily leaned up on her side. "Will you stay tonight?"

"Of course, unless you planned on throwing me out," Rachel said, getting back into bed. Rachel brushed back Lily's hair and stared deeply into her eyes.

"You feel good," Rachel said, squeezing her.

"So do you," Lily responded, reaching for Rachel.

"You're going to be awfully tired in the morning."

"I don't care."

Rachel woke up to the sound of the shower. Lily came out naked with a towel wrapped around her head. She sat on the edge of the bed and looked tentatively at Rachel.

"Are you sorry?"

"Sorry about what?"

"About last night."

Rachel wrapped her arms around Lily's smooth waist, whiffing lotion and the faint scent of lavender.

"No. Are you?"

"It was kind of a surprise, but a nice surprise."

"Will you go to dinner with me tonight?" Rachel asked, kissing the back of Lily's neck.

"Does this mean we're dating?"

"Dating, mating, buying matching silverware. Will you relax? I want you. I need you. I like being with you. And believe it or not, I think about you a lot," Rachel said, wrestling her down in the bed. "And if you wouldn't be late for work, I'd seduce you all over again."

"Make me late."

Hope and Rachel stood across from each other at the kitchen island sipping coffee. They both had an odd glow about them.

"So," Hope said.

"So. How was your evening?" Rachel asked, thinking about her own.

"Nice, and yours?" Hope asked, wondering if Rachel knew she hadn't come home.

"Good, very good."

"Theirs must have been fantastic. They're still in bed. I hope we're like them when we're older."

"With the right partners," Rachel said. "You never know. You look good. You have good color, weight, smiling eyes. I'm glad you came out for the summer."

Hope put her arm around Rachel's shoulder. "So am I. Rach, what am I going to do about Pamela?"

"I don't know. But I think I'm going to have to transfer schools. If I hadn't brought you, this wouldn't be happening. That's exactly how Pamela is going to see it."

"No, she'll think you had it planned all along."

"Maybe she won't take it that hard," Rachel said.

Hope looked at her with a raised eyebrow.

"You're right. She's gonna kill us both."

"It's going to be extremely unpleasant."

"That's putting it mildly. It's going to be a fucking disaster."

"Summer's not over yet. Maybe we could just not think about it for a while."

"Good idea," Rachel said.

"Has something happened to you recently?" Hope asked. She had been expecting a lecture on procrastination and what a mess of things she was making.

"No, why?"

"You seem unusually relaxed."

"I think I'm happy."

"Good."

"Are you happy?"

"I'm very happy," Hope said.

* * * * *

127

Later that night while she was sitting in the park with Emerson, she thought about their conversation.

"Emerson, are you happy?"

"I'm fucking ecstatic."

"Really?"

"Yes, darling, I'm very happy. I'm scared, but I'm happy."

"Scared?"

"You know, all those growing pains we have to go through."

Hope saw two older women meeting each other across the park. They embraced and kissed each other quickly. Hope didn't think anything of it. The town was full of gays and lesbians for the festival weekend.

She had sat outside the café earlier and watched them come and go all day. There was an amazing assortment, but none quite so stunning in Hope's eyes as Emerson coming across the square to meet her for lunch. She experienced that feeling again of love rushes and marveled at it.

"Guess who that is across the way," Emerson said.

"Who?"

"Ruthie Clark and Elise. Somebody's going to be in trouble when the wife gets wind of it."

"What's the deal with those two?"

"In and out of love for years. Ruthie played around a lot when she was younger. Dated half the women in town. Broke Elise's heart, and that's where Sal came in. Sal was stable. She wanted a wife and the home-on-the-range scene. Elise needed that. Still, she always had a penchant for Ruthie. Never really got over it. Ruthie started to slow down, and she's been after Elise ever since."

"So that day in the café . . . ?"

"Yeah, that's been going on forever too. Sal knows that Elise can't get Ruthie out of her system. You know it's weird, but love really can be like a drug. A needle in the vein, and you can't control it. Fall for somebody hard, and recovery's a bitch."

"Is that what Angel is to you? A needle to the vein?"

"Yes and no. I think it took you for me to be over her. What about you and Pamela?"

"I'm not sure what to feel. I guess it still seems abstract. It probably will until I tell her I'm in love with you."

"Are you sad about leaving her?"

"I don't know. It's such a strange thing. Maybe I've been falling out of love for a while and that makes it hurt less. Maybe being in love with you makes me not want to think about it."

"You're not sorry you're in love with me, are you?"

"No, I'm fucking ecstatic that I'm in love with you," Hope said, rolling on top of Emerson. "Now take me home and make love to me."

"Gladly, my darling."

Emerson disentangled herself from Hope in the middle of the night to look out the window, trying to figure out what all the ruckus was about. She'd heard sirens. Up the hillside she could see a raging fire. Smoke billowed into the night air, clouding over the moon like the earth smoking a cigarette and blowing it into the light of a single, naked bulb. Hope leaned up, sleepy and tousled.

"Emerson?"

"There's a fire, a big fire. Looks like it's on Fourteenth Street. I've got to go see. This is scary."

"I'll come with you."

"You don't have to," Emerson said, sitting on the edge of the bed and shoving her sneakers on.

"I want to," Hope said, taking her hand.

They found half the town standing in front of the house. The windows filled with blazing red. Ruthie Clark stood next to Elise, holding her hand, tears streaming down her face.

"Why?" Elise asked.

"Because she's a vindictive bitch," Ruthie said.

Hope and Emerson joined Katherine and Berlin.

"Sal burned down the house. She's threatened to do it for years. Well, she finally did it," Berlin told them.

"She didn't want Elise to have anything, so she torched it," Katherine said.

"I'll buy you new things, sweetheart," Ruthie said, pulling Elise tight.

"Where's Sal?" Emerson asked.

"In jail. They're taking this pretty seriously," Katherine said.

"What? You can't burn down your own house?" Emerson said.

"Not if it endangers the rest of the town," Katherine said.

Hope took Emerson's hand, praying this wasn't

some kind of omen to her own love affair's demise. She had been hoping that all would go smoothly, that Pamela would act like a lady and know when to leave. Now she was having second thoughts. Wives burning down houses frightened her.

"Shit, this looks good. Fine weekend to do it. Of course it'll be all over the papers. People in Grover's Corner ought to love this. I can see the headline now, OUT-OF-CONTROL LESBIAN TRIES TO BURN TOWN," Berlin said.

"Berlin, you're not being very supportive. Sal was obviously distraught or she wouldn't have done this," Katherine said.

"It's perfectly understandable to be distraught. It's psychotic to burn down your house and everything in it," Berlin replied.

Rachel came flying up the hill and was dumbstruck.

She leaned toward Hope. "Pamela doesn't like matches, does she?"

Hope looked over at Rachel queerly. She had read her mind.

"Lots of people break up and don't do this," Emerson said, putting a protective arm around Hope. Still, thoughts of her own behavior at being dumped contained the same psychotic elements. What was Pamela Severson capable of? Was she capable of winning Hope back?

Ruthie led Elise away from the fire. The townspeople looked on sympathetically.

"Should've married a man. A man wouldn't burn your house down for playing around. He'd knock you upside the head instead," Dickie Sharp bellowed out. He took a swig from a bottle of Jack Daniel's. He

131

didn't see Emerson coming. She kicked him hard in the groin. He spat liquor everywhere and went down hugging his balls.

Emerson took Hope's hand, smiled sweetly at Katherine, and walked off.

"You've got to love her," Berlin said. "That girl has balls."

"Let's hope they're big enough to stand up to Pamela," Rachel said.

"I really must meet this woman you all are so afraid of. Does she resemble Medusa in any way?" Berlin said.

"She's got a different hairdo," Rachel replied.

Twelve

Emerson looked out the window. She had been studying the sketches of Hope that covered the wall. She couldn't decide which one she would sculpt. Her first piece using Hope as her model would be sacred, and she wanted to make certain she did it right. This wasn't going to be just any piece of sculpture. This was the woman she loved. Desperately, as she was discovering. She swallowed hard at the task. It seemed she'd have a lifetime project doing all the sides of Hope. She prayed she'd be granted such a wish.

But instead of working, Emerson was thinking about how much she missed Hope. She had gone to Grover's Corner with Berlin and Rachel. They were shopping for Katherine's birthday present and other essentials for the party. Berlin was planning a surprise birthday party, and Hope and Rachel had been drafted as her assistants. The day lingered endlessly before her. Emerson kept reminding herself that she was supposed to be working.

She didn't regret falling love. It had happened so easily that she hadn't even thought about it. That was the best kind of love she supposed. Only her girlfriend wasn't a girlfriend; she was a mistress, and off somewhere in the wings was a wife.

Rachel had told Emerson that if Hope didn't go back, her academic career was finished. Pamela would see to that. She was in a position to do it. But Hope told Emerson she didn't want to get her doctorate. For now at least, Emerson thought. But what about later?

The uncertain future tormented Emerson. It was mid-August, and in six weeks all would have to be decided. Was it fair to ask Hope to give up years of study and her career? And what would she be getting in return? A crazy artist who lived like a transient in a dilapidated brick building.

Emerson couldn't get the feeling out of her head that maybe she was only summertime fun and then when it was over there would be no bouncing back from this one. That would be just what Hope needed, knowing that she'd sent someone around the bend.

Emerson pressed her head against the window.

Why is everything good outlined with something very bad?

She heard soft footsteps running up the stairs. Her heart leaped as Hope burst into the room.

She took Emerson in her arms and squeezed her tight.

"I've been thinking about you all day. I bought you a present," Hope said, pulling out a Saint Christopher's medallion and putting it around Emerson's neck.

Emerson looked down at it.

"It's to keep you safe when I'm not around to protect you."

Emerson got a queer look on her face.

"Which won't be very often, I hope. Darling, you look like you've been fretting about something. What's wrong?"

"Nothing really. I can't decide which one of you to do," Emerson said, pointing to the wall of sketches.

"You'll figure it out, being the artistic genius you are," Hope said, kissing Emerson's neck, slowly unbuttoning her shirt, and then running her tongue along the top of her shorts. She undid them and took Emerson in her mouth. Emerson closed her eyes, ran her fingers through Hope's hair, and felt things she didn't think herself capable of.

Later, as they lay among the clothes on the unmade bed, Hope apologized. "I can't seem to get enough of you. I shouldn't be so forward."

Emerson looked over at her, and tears welled up in her eyes.

"What's wrong? Did I hurt you?"

Emerson pulled Hope close.

"Why are you sad?" Hope said, wiping tears from those beautiful blue eyes and looking thoroughly alarmed.

"I think I love you too much, and I'm frightened that if you go away I won't be able to stand it," Emerson finally answered.

"And where would I be going?"

"Back to New York."

"Why?"

"Because that's where you live," Emerson responded.

"But I don't have to live there. I kind of thought I'd hang out with you. I'll find a place here," Hope said, brushing Emerson's hair back from her face.

"You're going to stay?"

"Of course, silly. What did you think I was going to do?"

"I don't know."

"Is that what's bothering you?"

"Yes."

"I love you. I know I've got some loose ends, but it doesn't mean I can't tidy them up a bit," Hope said, running her finger around Emerson's nipple.

"I could buy a house," Emerson offered.

"And why would you want to do that?" Hope asked, taking Emerson's nipple in her mouth.

"So we'd have a place to live."

"You might have to talk me into that," Hope said, sliding on top of Emerson. Feeling her inside, she smiled.

"And how might I do that?" Emerson asked, pulling away.

"Come back . . ." Hope pleaded.

"Will you live with me?"

"Yes," Hope said, closing her eyes.

Rachel sat across the table from Hope and Emerson. She could tell Emerson had been crying. She watched Hope touch Emerson's cheek, as if to reassure her. They'd been noticeably late for dinner. Rachel added this up to something gone awry, and she didn't like it.

Berlin and Katherine were still trying to decide where in Europe their trip would take place. And then there was the café. Someone needed to oversee things, and at the moment their current help was less than ideal.

"Rachel, when are you going back?" Katherine asked, as she passed the almond cheese soufflé to Emerson.

Berlin glared at her. "Don't muck it up this time, Emerson. Remember how I showed you to serve it."

"I won't," Emerson said. "I am becoming less of a savage if you haven't noticed."

"I've got to leave by the fifteenth of September at the very latest," Rachel said, pouring herself another glass of wine. She wished Lily could have come, but there'd been a problem with one of the concession tents, and she had to stay. Rachel was slightly bruised from their afternoon romping. She still had that glow about her of being freshly fucked.

"Too soon," Berlin said. "I can't be organized enough by then."

"Shit," Katherine said.

"We'll figure something out," Berlin said.

"Why don't you show me what to do and I'll watch it? Emerson can help me if I get stuck," Hope said.

They all turned to look at her. Emerson opened her eyes big, twisted her mouth, and looked horribly guilty.

"You're not coming back with me?" Rachel asked.

"No, I'm not," Hope said, pouring herself another glass of wine and looking across the table to what appeared as a viable imitation of the Spanish Inquisition.

"What about school?" Rachel asked.

"I've had enough of that for a while. Peas, anyone?" Hope said, passing them to her left.

"Just like that, you're throwing everything to the four winds and you're going to stay in this little hick town and do what?" Rachel said, her voice getting higher.

"I was thinking of raising chickens," Hope said.

"Chickens?" Berlin said.

"I don't know. Something. I'm sure I'll find something to do. Actually, I kind of like the idea of not having a plan. I've never done that before, and I'd like to try it."

"Good for you, Hope," Katherine said. "You can stay here as long as you like, really."

"I'm going to buy a house," Emerson said, "and she's coming to live with me."

"What!" Rachel said, standing up. "Has everyone lost their fucking minds?"

"Rachel, darling, sit down. It's most impolite to

stand at the dinner table," Katherine said, patting Rachel's vacant chair.

"Hope, let's be realistic here. I know that you have become quite attached to Emerson, but giving up everything you've worked for to stay here because of your current infatuation is not a good idea."

"It's a little more than an infatuation, Rachel," Emerson said, her face beginning to flush.

"You two have been dating for the minor part of a summer. I hardly think that warrants asking someone to give up her life," Rachel screeched.

"I didn't ask her to give up anything," Emerson replied.

"Rachel, calm down," Katherine said, trying to take her hand. Rachel pulled it away.

"I don't want to calm down. Hope, what are you going to do? Call Pamela and say 'Guess what, I'm not coming back,' " Rachel said.

"Yes, that is exactly what I'm going to do."

"You can't just do that," Rachel said.

"Yes, I can. Rachel, what did you think? That I was just playing around with Emerson, that when the summer ended we'd say good-bye, thanks for the good time. It's more than that. I love her, and I intend to spend a good portion of my life with her, fate willing," Hope said.

Emerson beamed.

"You two are fucking crazy. You just met. You can't just run off and get married."

"Why not?" Berlin asked.

"Because it's not right. It's not supposed to happen like that. Relationships take planning and time, and because I didn't bring you here to lose you," Rachel said, staring at Hope. She felt tears building up. She looked at both her friends and then ran from the room. She walked out of the house, tears streaking her face.

"It must be Clifford's genes bringing out this analytical, hopelessly unromantic side of Rachel. It couldn't possibly be something out of me. And it wasn't nurture. Katherine, what have we done wrong to bring up such a rotten little lesbian?" Berlin said, replenishing everyone's wine.

"Berlin, that's not nice," Katherine said.

"Why is she so angry?" Hope asked. "We talked about me leaving Pamela. I didn't think this would come as such a surprise."

Katherine met Berlin's gaze. She shrugged her shoulders.

"Tell her," Berlin said.

"Hope, I think Rachel is rather, how would you say it, enamored with you," Katherine said.

Hope was silent for a moment. "But I never thought of her that way or felt that way. What did she think I was doing with Emerson?"

"Playing around, I think," Katherine responded.

"Well it's more than that," Hope said, feeling her face get hot. She was confused.

"I know. It's just one of those things," Katherine said.

Emerson took her hand.

That night as Emerson and Hope lay in bed, Emerson looked over at her. Stroking her cheek, she asked, "Are you sure you want to stay here? I could go anywhere with you."

"I like it here. I've lived in big cities my whole life. I'd like to try this. Emerson, don't worry. It's all right. I've thought about what I'm doing. I want to stay here."

Rachel found Hope alone in the morning. Hope was dressed in one of Emerson's long shirts, reading a book and drinking coffee. She appeared perfectly content and relaxed. Rachel felt haggard. She couldn't sleep. She was embarrassed about making such a scene, and she worried what Hope might be thinking.

Sheepishly, she looked around for Emerson.

"She's not here. She's meeting with Lauren. Rachel, are you all right?" Hope asked, cocking her head to one side.

"I'm sorry about last night," Rachel said, taking a chair next to Hope.

"Nothing to be sorry about. I meant to tell you. We had just decided what to do and out it came at dinner. I know you think this is fast, but I'd like to give it a go. I can't go back. I can't even see myself going back. It almost seems like it was someone else's life."

"I'm going to miss you," Rachel said, feeling herself getting teary.

"I'm going to miss you too," Hope said, giving her a hug, "but I'll be here when you come home. Besides, I think you'll be spending some time with someone else. And that's good. That's what you need to be doing."

"I know," Rachel said, remembering that her mother had said Hope wasn't hers to have.

Rachel walked over to the large piece in the corner. "Is she going to be ready for the show?"

"She wants to do one more piece," Hope said.

"And let me guess who it's of," Rachel said, smiling. "You've done wonders for each other."

"Isn't that what love is supposed to do?" Hope said, taking Rachel's hand.

"So you're really going to call Pamela and say good-bye?"

"Something like that. I think I'll tell her I've fallen in love with someone else. I'm sorry, but there's no remedy. What can she do? I hardly think she'd come fetch me."

Rachel raised an eyebrow.

"She wouldn't, would she?"

"Naw, she may be aggressive, but I don't think she'd do that."

"Can we be certain?"

"We'd hide you," Rachel assured her.

Emerson came flying up the stairs and swooped Hope up in her arms.

"Hi, Rach," Emerson said beaming.

It was hard not to be happy when her two best friends were madly in love. Rachel gave them both a gentle shove and went off to work. There was nothing quite like a happy ending, Rachel thought as she walked to the café.

Katherine and Berlin stared at her tentatively from around the kitchen at the café.

"Stop doing that. I'm all right. I'm over it," Rachel said.

They came out to check.

"Are you sure?" Katherine asked.

"Yes, I'm sure. I went to talk to Hope. They're so fucking happy it's sickening. Even I can't deny they make a darling couple," Rachel said, picking up a stack of menus.

Berlin smiled.

"And yes, you were right," Rachel said, swinging her arm around Berlin's shoulders.

"So all we have to get through is the divorce," Berlin said.

"Divorces can be messy," Katherine said.

"This one won't be," Rachel said.

"I wouldn't be so sure," Berlin said.

"What makes you say that?" Rachel asked.

"I'm getting bad vibes about this one," Berlin replied.

"Did your Ouija board predict blood?"

"No. I just don't think it's going to be easy as Hope wants it to be," Berlin said. "Good-byes are never easy, and they're never simple."

"I guess we'll just have to see," Rachel said, heading off in the direction of customers.

Thirteen

Hope modeled, and Emerson worked frantically. Emerson desperately wanted her piece of Hope to be in the show. It seemed to signify their bargain, their beginning a new life together. When it was cast and finished, Emerson invited Berlin, Katherine, Rachel, and Lily over for wine, cheese, and the unveiling.

"Goodness, now she's throwing parties," Berlin said, holding the invitation in her hand.

"She has come a long way," Katherine said, turning the barbecued chicken over on the grill.

"The civilizing effects of love," Berlin murmured, obviously musing back to some other time and place.

"Yes. I wonder who that reminds you of," Katherine said, closing the lid on the barbecue.

Berlin handed her a beer and pulled out a chair for her.

"You're such a gentlewoman, such manners," Katherine said.

"I learned it all from you," Berlin replied.

"No, you learned it in prep school, but you conveniently forgot when you became a wild lesbian about town."

"We all go through changes. God, those were fun days."

"And what are they now?" Katherine said, pursing her lips in a pout.

"Now they're wonderful. I have had the best times of my life with you," Berlin said, putting her arms around Katherine. "I wouldn't trade it for anything."

"People think we're antediluvians, you know," Katherine said.

"So? I like that. We're slowly becoming lesbian icons. Someone's got to prove to these youngsters that longevity has its benefits. You can't always go flitting from mountaintop to mountaintop and never experience what's below. You've got to go through things together, even dreaded boredom, to come out stronger and fitter than when you went in," Berlin said.

"You should become a counselor," Katherine said, pinching her.

"Oh no, no headshrinker here. Besides, Lutz

accused me of having a gambling problem at poker the other night. She said I was compulsive," Berlin said, furrowing her brow.

"You are."

"No, I just like to do it, and I'm good at it. We haven't lost the house yet, have we? Everyone has a thing."

"A fetish or two. Was Lutz winning or losing when she said this?"

"Losing. She always loses because she's cocky. I stop when I am not having a good night. Or I stay low. Lutz insists on taunting fate. If fate decides that tonight is not your night, you need to accept it and move on. Lutz thinks if you throw money at her, fate will change her mind. Not so."

"Not only are you smart, you're sexy," Katherine said, getting up to check the chicken and swatting Berlin on the rear as she passed.

Berlin picked up a dish towel and snapped her back.

Katherine waved a long grill fork at her. Berlin picked up the equally long tongs.

They were fencing when Rachel and Lily found them out back. Rachel rolled her eyes at Lily. Sometimes her mothers embarrassed her.

"Will they ever grow up?" Rachel asked.

"I hope not," Lily said, taking her hand. "They're full of joie de vivre. It's a good thing, Rachel. You have it down deep. I know you do."

"You'll have to be the one to bring it bubbling to the surface," Rachel said.

"And I intend to," Lily said, taking the beer that Rachel offered her.

"Where are Hope and Emerson?" Katherine asked.

"They can't come. They rented a truck and are going to the foundry in Grover's Corner to pick up the statue. They're too busy for us now, I guess," Rachel said.

"Rachel, that's not nice. Emerson is excited about this show. Don't be a spoilsport," Katherine said.

"Yeah, don't be such a spoilsport," Lily said, picking up a dish towel and snapping it at Rachel. Rachel grabbed another, and soon a war had begun.

"Dish towels lying around just seem to inspire that," Berlin said.

"Kids these days," Katherine said, smiling as Lily and Rachel crashed to the ground, rolling around on the grass.

Emerson finished unpacking it. Hope stood back.

"It's beautiful, Emerson, absolutely beautiful."

"That's because you're beautiful," Emerson said, standing back.

"It's a good thing you got the freight elevator fixed or she'd be living downstairs," Hope said.

"She turned out all right," Emerson said, surveying her from all sides.

"Let me get this straight, though. We brought her here, but we have to move all of them back to Grover's Corner for the show."

"I like to have them around me until they find homes. It's my mothering instinct. She stays, however," Emerson said.

"You're not going to sell it?"

"Not even to the highest bidder. This one is mine."

147

"That's sweet, Emerson, but you don't have to do that. You'll make more."

"I know, but this one's special. They're all special," Emerson said, looking around the room at her most recent works. "But I get to keep some. And she's one of them."

"And what do the kept ones mean?"

"I don't know for sure. It's a feeling, I guess. Something special goes on in my life then, and it comes out just a little better than all the rest."

"Where's the one of Angel?" Hope asked, suddenly noticing she was gone. Hope had sometimes sat with Angel when Emerson was gone. She kept looking at her, trying to figure out the woman who inspired the piece. It was an incredible work.

"I sold it."

"You sold it! Why? To whom?"

"I sold her because I don't need her anymore, and the person I sold it to needed it more. She doesn't know that I know she bought it. Lauren wasn't supposed to tell me."

"Who bought it?"

"Angel's mother."

"She misses her?"

"Badly."

"That was nice, Emerson."

"I'm happy now. It's not hard to give someone else something when I'm happy."

"Still, you're a sweet woman."

"Remember that the next time you're mad at me."

"Have I ever been mad at you?"

"Not yet. But you will."

"Does that worry you?"

"No. It's part of it, isn't it? Little domestic squabbles mean you're in love."

"We have a lot ahead of us," Hope said, suddenly feeling the gravity of starting a new life with a new person. They'd moved Hope's favorite chair, her father's chair, into the studio. Emerson served her up a scotch as Hope eased back into her chair. Emerson sat back and admired her.

It was a first step but an easy one, a tentative one, like when Hope first moved clothes into Pamela's. It wasn't until summer when Hope was out of the dorm that Pamela persuaded her to stay in the city instead of going home. Moving in was serious, and it made Hope nervous.

"Don't be scared. We already spend a lot of time together. I promise not to turn into a monster," Emerson said, taking her hand.

"I know. I'm sorry. I worry that I'm capable of failure now. I never had a string of failed relationships behind me. But now I do. I'm divorced. I have a marriage behind me. I have failed."

"So have I. So what? We're not perfect. We learned things, didn't we?"

"I hope so."

"We're older now."

"Been through a few more hoops," Hope said.

"Exactly. Maybe now we know what not to do. Weren't you the one who told me not to give up on love? It seems to me you're the one with the bad attitude now."

"Bad or realistic," Hope said.

"You're getting cold feet. I knew this would happen," Emerson said, looking at Hope. She stormed out of the room.

"Emerson, wait!"

The door slammed. Hope stood for a moment. Am I getting cold feet? she asked herself. No. I'm anticipating a disaster before it happens, and so what if it does. I love her now. And now is all that matters. Hope ran up the stairs to the living quarters. Emerson had locked the door.

"Emerson, open the door, please. I'm sorry. I'm scared, that's all. It doesn't mean I don't want it. It doesn't mean I don't want you."

"You lied," Emerson screamed from behind the door.

"How did I lie?"

"It is just a summertime fling. That's all you want it to be."

"No, it's not. I love you, dammit. Now open the fucking door."

"Don't scream obscenities at me."

"I love you. Please don't do this to me," Hope said, sliding to the floor.

"Do what? You're the one who wants out."

"I don't. I swear it. Emerson, I want to talk to you, not this door. Please."

"No. Just go away."

"I can't go away. I love you."

Hope buried her head and cried.

Emerson opened the door.

"Don't cry. Please don't cry," Emerson said, putting her arms around Hope.

Hope looked up. Emerson wiped away her tears.

"I'm sorry," Emerson said.

"You're not a fling."

"Okay."

"Do you believe me?"

"I believe you."

"I got scared."

"I'm scared too."

"I think we just had our first argument," Hope said.

"Speak of the devil, huh," Emerson said, helping Hope up.

She took Hope in her arms.

"I love you too much. I can't help feeling that this is too good to be true. Maybe sometimes I'm just waiting for you say it's over because that's what I expect," Emerson said.

"I feel the same way. Good things can be just as frightening as bad things."

"And then we have Rachel, who makes it sound like you can't fall madly in love in a summer."

"And an ex-wife who doesn't know she is one yet," Hope added on.

"Yeah. No wonder we're nervous. Speaking of that, when are you going to tell her?"

"How about tonight after a scotch?" Hope said.

"I'm not pressuring you."

"I know."

"Let's not fight anymore, okay?"

"Not for tonight at least. We're going to have squabbles you know."

"I know."

"Do you always run off and lock the door?" Hope asked.

"Yes."

"It's hard to have a discussion that way."

"I know."

"Can we talk about things next time?"

"With the door open?"

"Yes, with the door open."

"I'll try."

"That's all I ask."

"Do we get to kiss and make up now?"

"Yes."

Emerson lay with her arm across Hope's stomach, her head nestled beneath Hope's chin.

"We can argue more often if it means we get to do this afterward," Emerson said.

"We already do this a lot," Hope said, stroking Emerson's hair.

"What voracious appetites we have."

"Do you think we'll grow out of it?"

"Not if I can help it."

"Berlin and Katherine still make love a lot," Hope said.

"Sign of a good love affair," Emerson replied, leaning over and kissing Hope's nipple.

"Or a sign of its demise."

"There you go again. What did she do to you?"

Hope thought for a moment. "She left me alone too long and too much. And when she did come around, it was always on her terms."

"I'm not that kind of lover," Emerson said, seriousness clouding her face.

"I know. Let's have a scotch and call her."

"Right now?" Emerson said, rolling Hope on her stomach and kissing her back.

"Well . . ."

* * * * *

"Are you ready?" Emerson asked, plugging in the phone.

Hope sat in her chair with a scotch in her hand. "I think so."

Emerson handed her the phone.

Hope's heart pounded in her head. She wiped her hands on her shorts and dialed the number. She had tried to rehearse what she would say. It always came out wrong. In actuality, she knew she'd blurt out the truth and let Pamela take it where she would. Hope didn't know what to expect.

She got the answering machine. She didn't leave a message. Instead, she called the school. Dr. Severson wasn't in, the receptionist told her.

"Will she be in tomorrow?"

"She's at a conference in New Mexico. Gallup, to be exact. She'll be back Monday."

Hope put the receiver down. She turned pale.

"What's wrong?"

"She's here."

"Who's here? Pamela?"

"She's in Gallup."

"A short drive."

"Exactly."

"Should we hide you?"

"No. I hadn't counted on face-to-face."

"In the long run it's better."

"You don't know Pamela."

"No. I don't. I don't think she's going to like me."

"No, she's not."

Fourteen

Rachel came running up the stairs to fetch Hope.

"Oh my god! You'll never believe who's here," Rachel said, out of breath. "Hope, it's awful."

"May I have another scotch?" Hope said, holding out her glass.

"I think you'll need one. If I drank, I'd need one," Emerson said.

"Hope, she's here, in our house, in the living room, wondering where you are."

"I know."

"How'd you know?"

"I called. They said she was here."

"What are you going to do?"

"Tell her the truth."

"This is going to be awful," Rachel said, her face beginning to flush.

"Emerson, pour Rachel a scotch. She needs one."

Rachel sat on a stool. Emerson handed her a glass and filled it.

"Hope, this is not good."

"Doesn't Emerson look good?" Hope said, straightening her collar and putting a stray curl back behind her ear.

"This is not the time to be admiring your mistress when the wife's in town. How can you be so calm?"

"Because getting upset isn't going to change anything. Besides, tonight is Emerson's big night, and I'm not about to let Pamela spoil it," Hope said, surveying Emerson again. "I think the whole black-white thing works well for you. Damn, you're cute."

"Thank you," Emerson said.

"You two are fucking crazy. We're on the verge of a crisis, and you act like nothing's wrong."

"Another scotch?" Emerson asked Hope, who nodded in Rachel's direction.

"What are you going to do?"

"Rachel, you're making things difficult. I am going to go with you, talk to Pamela most cordially, go to the opening, and then afterward tell her about Emerson. It's simple, and it will work."

"You're being way too optimistic."

"Relax, Rachel. Now, Emerson, no getting messy until Lauren comes to get you. Promise?"

"I promise. Are you sure you're going to be all right?"

"Yes, darling. Now kiss me."

"You really think you can just tell her and, like that, it's over?" Rachel asked as they walked across town.

Hope looked over at her and smiled.

"Oh my god, you're drunk. I should have known. You've been sitting there getting drunk, knowing someone would come fetch you when she got here."

Hope smiled and said nothing.

"How many have you had?"

"Six," Hope said.

"Have you ever had six scotches in a row before?"

"No."

"This is going to be good."

"We'll laugh about it later, I'm sure."

"You don't feel sick, do you?"

"No, I feel wonderful."

"Okay."

Hope weaved a little now and then, but over all she did well until she tripped coming up the stairs to the house, skinning her knees and hitting her chin. Berlin and Pamela heard the commotion and came outside.

Hope was laughing hysterically and holding her shins. Her chin was bleeding. Rachel was desperately trying to collect her, but she was too late.

Hope looked up at Pamela. "Hi there. Did you have a nice trip?"

"I should ask you the same thing," Pamela said,

helping her up. Pamela drew her near and smelled alcohol. "You've been drinking."

"I have."

Berlin guided Rachel into the house and left them alone.

"She's not going to tell her now. After the opening," Rachel whispered.

"She doesn't think anything is going on."

"She'll find out soon enough. Where's Mom?"

"Upstairs, putting on the final touches," Berlin said.

"I've really missed you," Pamela said and then kissed Hope deeply.

"We really shouldn't be doing that," Hope said, looking into those pale, gray eyes.

"Why not?"

"I'll tell you later."

"So we're going to an art opening?"

"Yep."

"And this Emerson is a friend of yours?"

"Yes."

"Rachel says one of the pieces in it is of you?"

"Yep."

"So you modeled for her . . . naked?"

"That's usually how it's done."

"It seems so out of character for you."

"A lot of things have changed, Pamela."

"I know. It's been a long summer. I can't wait for you to come back. Aside from being a little tanked, you look wonderful."

"I feel better. I've had a wonderful summer."

"I'm glad."

"I think I need to clean up my wounds," Hope said, smiling rather wistfully at Pamela. Maybe this wsn't going to be as easy as she thought.

"Ouch!" Hope screeched as Rachel put hydrogen peroxide on her chin.

Pamela looked on, sipped her wine, and chatted amiably with Katherine about must-see sights in Europe.

"You didn't tell her anything, did you?" Rachel whispered, looking over Hope's shoulder at Pamela.

"No, not yet. I'm not going to have to wear a Band-Aid? I'll look perfectly ridiculous."

"That should be the least of your worries right now."

"You're right. It's not going to be easy."

"You'll get through it. You're not going to change your mind, are you?"

"Hell no!"

Her emphatic display brought attention. Pamela looked at her quizzically. Berlin and Katherine made quick eye contact.

"Perhaps we should go," Katherine suggested.

"Are we still picking up Lily?" Berlin asked Rachel.

"No, she's going to meet us there. She's coming later."

"Lily?" Pamela asked.

"Rachel's summertime romance," Hope chided.

"New girlfriends are nice. I look forward to meeting her," Pamela said.

"Oh, you'll meet more than one new girlfriend tonight," Rachel replied.

Pamela looked at her queerly while Hope smiled benignly.

"Let's go," Katherine said.

When they arrived, Emerson watched Hope tentatively from across the room.

"You're not listening to me," Lauren said, grabbing Emerson's head and looking intently at her.

"I'm listening," Emerson replied, looking intently at Hope.

"No, you're staring at your girlfriend."

"Don't say it so loud."

"Why not?"

"The woman standing next to her is her wife."

"That figures. You finally found someone that's good for you, and she's married. How's that going to work out?"

"In my favor, I hope."

"So do I," Lauren said, studying Pamela Severson. She looked like a woman who got her way.

Pamela moved around the room, studying all the pieces, until she came to the one of Hope. She smiled at the figure and looked over at Hope. "It appears you've spent the summer becoming immortalized in bronze. She did you justice," Pamela said, taking Hope's hand in hers.

Hope smiled weakly and looked over at Emerson. This is not going well, she thought. She could tell that Emerson was getting nervous and was close to becoming distraught.

"I've missed you," Pamela said, stroking Hope's cheek.

"Pamela, we need to talk about some things."

"I know, sweetheart, but let's have fun tonight. We've got the fall to straighten things around. I know that I let stuff slip between us, but I think being apart helped me realize that you are very important to me. I don't want to lose you," Pamela said, encircling her and holding her tight.

Hope looked over her shoulder and saw Emerson standing across the room looking mortified. Emerson turned and left.

Hope disentangled herself from Pamela and ran after Emerson, leaving Pamela rather stunned. Rachel saw everything and went over to distract Pamela.

Emerson stood in the empty hallway between galleries. She was shaking. Hope closed the door and took her in her arms.

"It will be over tonight. I promise. Don't let her ruin your night."

"I don't care about tonight. I can't stand there and watch her with you ... doing those things. It's awful. She loves you. I can see it. We're going to destroy her life!"

"Emerson, calm down. I can't help it that I've fallen out of love with one woman and into love with another. It's more of a crime to stay with her, not loving her and pretending. It's going to hurt. I know that. But we've all had failed love affairs, and we all survive them. I'm not letting you go," Hope said, staring into her eyes. "I mean it."

Emerson kissed her, seeking reassurance with her body for the doubts raging through her mind. Hope reached for her, kissing her neck and ears, slowly unzipping her pants, and entering her. Emerson closed her eyes and let Hope quickly bring her to orgasm.

Emerson smiled and cooed love before she did likewise to Hope, who stood waiting and willing. When it was over they both stood breathless.

"I love you," Hope said.

"I know. I'm sorry."

"It'll all work out, okay?"

"Okay."

"How are you going to do this?"

"I don't know yet. Go somewhere and have a talk."

"Take the car and go out to Finson Road. It's quiet, and there won't be any distractions. It'll be easier on everyone. I wouldn't want to get dumped in front of an audience. Kinder that way," Emerson said, handing her the car keys. "Are you sure?"

"Sure about what?"

"About us."

Hope smiled at her. "Very sure. Don't worry, okay?"

Emerson held her hand, and they lingered for a moment.

"Let's go," Emerson said, straightening her shoulders.

Hope and Emerson walked back into the gallery. Pamela watched them. Lauren grabbed Emerson and brought her over to a prospective client.

Pamela looked at Hope queerly. "Is that the artist?"

"That's Emerson. Let's go talk."

"Are you all right? You're flushed," Pamela said, touching her cheek.

"I'm fine. Let's go."

"Where are we going?"

"For a drive."

"All right," Pamela said, allowing herself to be led out of the gallery.

Emerson watched them go.

"Whose car?" Pamela asked, as they got in the MG.

"Emerson's," Hope replied.

"It's nice. She must make some money."

"She does," Hope said, pulling away from the curb.

"So she's talented and rich?"

"Yes."

"And she's a friend and you posed for her nude and she lets you drive her car?"

"Yes."

"Are you sleeping with her?" Pamela asked.

Hope hit the highway, looked over at Pamela briefly, swallowed hard, and said, "Yes."

"That's what you wanted to talk about?"

"Yes."

Pamela sat quiet.

"Hope . . ."

"I'm sorry. I didn't mean for this to happen."

Hope turned off the freeway and drove up the hill to Finson Road. She parked the car and turned to look at Pamela, who sat staring off into space. Digesting facts, Hope supposed.

"What does this mean?" Pamela said, turning to look at her.

"That I'm leaving you," Hope replied.

"I could overlook this," Pamela replied.

"Overlook what?" Hope asked.

"A fling."

"It's not a fling."

"Hope, I know things haven't always been the best between us, but we can work them out. You're young. A little summer romance, an occasional straying . . . I can understand. I know you didn't have a lot of lovers before me. Things happen. It's not a big deal. You learned some things, had some fun. It's all right. Really. She's attractive. You did well. Someday, you can tell me all the lurid details."

"Pamela, it's not like that," Hope said, feeling suddenly helpless.

Pamela took Hope's face in her hands and kissed her. "I love you, darling, and I have no intention of letting you go. Rich and famous artist or no. You're mine."

"You can't own someone," Hope said, feeling exasperation creeping into her voice. "I'm fucking someone else. I love someone else. Doesn't that mean anything to you?"

"Yes. It means you're going through some growing pains. Really, darling. It's all right. I don't hold any grudges."

Hope got out of the car and leaned against the hood, incredulous. How do you deal with someone that won't let you go? She hadn't anticipated this. Tears, ravings, a few choice obscenities, but denial? She didn't know what to do. She heard the other car door shut and felt Pamela beside her.

"Nice moon," Pamela said.

Hope looked up at it.

"I'm not coming back. I'm going to live with Emerson."

"And do what? Throw your career away? I don't

163

think so. It's infatuation, Hope. We all suffer from it from time to time. You meet someone, she's new to your life, you find each other fascinating, you might sleep together, but it doesn't mean you give up your wife or the stable parts of your life. It's all right to have an occasional mistress, but you tire of them after a while. You'll see."

Hope met her gaze. "Have you had an occasional mistress since we've been together?"

"Of course, darling, but they never really meant anything. They were simply temporary distractions. You're the one I want to be with. Hope, we make a good couple. We work well together. Don't screw it up."

"I can't fucking believe you. I never operated under the principle that taking the odd lover was part of the bargain. So all those nights I waited for you, thinking you were working, you were off fucking someone else."

"Not all of them."

"Just some of them."

"Really, Hope, I wouldn't have told you, if I thought it would upset you like this. After all, I'm not the one who's fucking the artist here."

"It's about time I did a little fucking around, don't you think? I think it's my turn."

"Yes, I suppose it is."

"So, what, twelve more and we're even?"

"I hardly think so, Hope. Suffice it to say a few."

"Few is more than two."

"Don't be petty, Hope," Pamela said, reaching out for her.

Hope moved away. "Don't touch me!"

"Hope, calm down."

"I don't think so. I've spent, or rather wasted, three years of my life with you, thinking of us as a couple, working to make us one, and now I find out that I was just your steady fuck."

"You're getting way out of line here," Pamela said, her face getting red. She grabbed Hope's arm. "I never intended to leave you for any of those others, contrary to what you're proposing."

"What are you going to do? Hit me again?"

"No," Pamela said, letting go. "I just want to talk to you."

"We have nothing left to say."

"Don't be so extreme."

Hope looked at her and burst into tears. "I trusted you."

Pamela put her arms around Hope. "I'm sorry. I shouldn't have told you. But you see how easily it can happen. You've done the same thing with Emerson. It happens sometimes. But it doesn't mean anything."

Hope looked at her. "No, it does mean something."

"Darling, as you grow up you'll see," Pamela said, drawing her in close.

Hope broke away. "What about *love, honor,* and *trust*? Don't those things matter to you?"

"You forgot *obey,* darling," Pamela chided, pulling at Hope, thinking now would be a good time to seduce her wife, placate her back into love. "We can work through this. No more lovers on the side. I promise. Now come here."

"No," Hope screamed.

"Don't be a foolish, Hope."

"I'd rather be a fool and live honestly than subscribe to your fucked-up system." Hope took one last long look at her wife and went running down the dark hillside.

"Hope . . . where are you going?"

"As far away from you as I can possibly get!" Hope screamed.

Pamela Severson was at a loss for words, one of the few times in her life. She'll calm down by morning, Pamela thought, fishing about for the car keys. That was the only problem with having younger lovers. They were such idealists.

Hope ran until she was knocked flat by a small protruding tree branch, which she had miscalculated in her rage. She picked herself up and began to walk, trying to think. All this time I agonized with the guilt of committing an infidelity when it was quite all right, part of any relationship. This is insane. She's insane. What, being faithful is archaic now?

By the time she got to Emerson's, Hope was covered in dirt; she'd been crying, and she had the distinct look of having been dragged behind a car.

"My god, what did she do to you?" Emerson asked.

"You won't believe it."

"Did she hurt you?"

Hope looked down at herself. "No, I left her on Finson Road with the car. I walked. I had to get away from her. I'm sure she'll bring the car back."

"Fuck the car. Hope, you really shouldn't go tripping across the countryside in the middle of the night. It's not safe."

"It was more dangerous to stay with her. Oh, Emerson, it was awful," Hope said, bursting into tears.

Emerson held her. "C'mon, let's get you cleaned up, and then we'll talk about it."

As they lay in bed, Hope told Emerson the story.

"So this is no big deal?"

"Obviously not, since it's part of any good marriage. Emerson . . ."

"Yes?"

"I don't want us to be like that."

"We won't be. I promise. Let's rest, and we'll deal with her in the morning."

"I'm never speaking to her again."

"All right. I'll tell her to piss off for you."

"Thanks," Hope said, snuggling up to Emerson and quickly falling asleep in her arms.

Emerson lay awake, wondering what sort of a monster Pamela Severson was. Hope was the sweetest woman. How could she possibly have lived with such a strangely detached, amoral woman? A woman, it seemed to Emerson, quite incapable of love.

In the morning Emerson came face-to-face with Pamela Severson sitting alongside the MG and nonchalantly smoking a cigarette. She had gone out for milk and the paper, leaving Hope sleeping.

"I believe this is yours," Pamela said, dangling the keys.

"Yes," Emerson replied, taking the car keys.

"Is she with you?"

For half a second she hesitated.

"I guess that means yes. Is she all right?"

"She's sleeping."

"I need to talk to her."

"She says she doesn't want to talk to you."

"She's my wife, remember?"

"I never once forgot."

"I'll bet you didn't. Tasty little dish, isn't she?"

"Don't talk like that."

"Oh please don't tell me we've another incurable romantic on our hands. Look, Emerson, whatever has gone on this summer is done. She's coming back with me. There's nothing for her here except maybe a few tumbles between the sheets."

"It's a lot more than that."

"So you say. Tell her to call me when she gets up. Don't forget," Pamela said, sauntering off.

Emerson had to severely restrain herself from hauling off and smacking the insolent bitch. Instead, she slammed the front door, which echoed throughout the building. Hope was sitting up when she got there.

"I'm sorry."

"What's wrong?"

"Pamela brought the car back."

"Oh."

"She wants you to call her."

"I'm not going to."

"I told her that."

"What did she say?"

"She doesn't believe me. She thinks we have nothing more between us than a few good fucks."

"She would. Come here," Hope said, holding out her arms. "We're a lot more than that."

"I know," Emerson said, feeling tears. She was angry and scared.

"Don't cry. She's not going to win," Hope said, kissing away Emerson's tears as they fell.

"I'm sorry you're in the middle of this."

Emerson buried her head in Hope's neck and held her tight.

"I'm not letting you go. That woman is evil."

"I know. We'll figure something out."

"Car bomb?"

"There's an idea," Hope said, smiling.

Rachel came flying up the stairs.

"You two look like shit," Rachel said.

"Thanks, Rachel. We were counting on you for a little moral support," Emerson said.

"Hope, what happened to your face?"

"Tree branch. I didn't duck in time."

"It seems your wife has no intentions of leaving unless you go with her."

"She can have my room at the house."

"Hope, this is serious. What are you going to do?" Rachel said, going to the fridge and pulling out a soda.

"I'm not going with her. I can't seem to make her understand that. I didn't think I would be the distraught one here, but then who counted on Pamela thinking affairs on the side are just dandy! How can I convince her that I don't love her? I'm at a loss."

"Where's Berlin?" Emerson asked.

"At the café. Why?" Rachel asked.

"She'll know what to do," Emerson said. "Rachel, will you stay here with Hope. I wouldn't want Pamela carting her off while I'm gone. I won't be long."

* * * * *

Berlin poured Emerson a cup of coffee.

"What's she doing?"

"Reading, staying by the phone, and waiting expectantly," Berlin replied.

"Tell me this is bizarre."

"She doesn't want to let go. Would you? Think about how you love Hope. Could you just let her go? What about your behavior with Angel? You didn't let go so well."

Berlin poured herself a cup and sat down next to Emerson.

"Hope is going to have to talk to her. This hiding out business is not going to fly. The longer she waits, the worse it will be."

"I don't know how I'm going to talk Hope into that. She's furious. I'm not so sure I want her talking to Pamela. She's quite the formidable foe."

"This will definitely be a test of your love."

"I don't want any tests. I just want us to start our life together and leave off all this old stuff."

"That's not being realistic. Every love affair has its baggage."

"What was my mother like when you came back with Katherine?" Emerson asked, suddenly remembering that Berlin had once been the other woman.

"Cordial, well-behaved, the perfect lady. This is not to say it didn't hurt her, but she never let on. I don't know how you ended up being such a savage. If your mother had lived, you'd be a lot different."

"I wouldn't count on it. We'd have probably fought all the time. At least this way I shan't have to live with her disappointment."

"I don't think she would have been disappointed with you. I think she would have been proud. She loved the arts. She would have liked having an artist for a daughter, especially such a talented one," Berlin said, smiling warmly at Emerson.

"Yeah, right, and a lesbian and at the moment a wife-stealer. Berlin, what am I going to do?"

"You're going to have to wait and let Hope do it. She's the only one who can convince Pamela that it's over."

"I know. All right. I hope this works out."

"It will, sweetheart."

Berlin watched Emerson leave. She looked a lot like her mother. Berlin remembered the last time she had seen Sarah alive. How they had wondered who the baby would look like. But Sarah never got to see Emerson; she only got to dream about her. Berlin and Katherine watched her grow up. And that was sad. Got to be careful with the ones you love, you never know when you might lose them and all those things you wish you'd said quivered on your tongue for eternity. There were a hundred things she would have liked to have told Sarah.

Berlin shrugged it off, thinking instead that her new house guest was beginning to prove taxing already. Thank god, Katherine was good at things like this. Berlin's lack of tact had got them into trouble more than once.

Pamela was so certain she could win Hope back that Berlin had to suppress the urge to slap her back into some sense of reality. The girl was really proving rather tedious. How could anyone be so certain of another's love to think that as soon as you walk into the picture your mere presence is enough to draw the other back? Frightening egoism.

Fifteen

Berlin and Katherine sat drinking coffee at the kitchen table, pretending they were not eavesdropping on Pamela's telephone conversation.

"It'll be by the end of the week, I'm sure. In the meantime, I need you to fax me some things. I'll send a list. There's a fax at one of the copy centers in this godforsaken little town. Hardly anything else," Pamela said, twirling a pencil and listening to her secretary rattle off duties, appointments, and such to her preoccupied boss. Pamela was not quite herself.

This thing with Hope was beginning to bother her. She half listened to Cybil and absentmindedly responded. She was really wondering where Hope was and what she was doing.

She had missed her this summer. Though she'd had an occasional afternoon romp, she had missed coming home to Hope. It was strange having grown used to someone who cared, someone who said *I love you* just when you needed to hear it, someone who held you. Having someone love you was different from being with someone who admired you or whom you challenged intellectually or who thought you were sexy after several glasses of wine at dinner and knew you wouldn't see each other until the next conference, and that was fine. That was understood.

Why had she told Hope about her other liaisons? That was truly stupid. Pamela did not do many stupid things, but that had been one blunder she would not easily repair. But she had thought it would bring Hope around, make her understand that sleeping with someone else did not mean she had to leave.

The difficulty was getting to Hope. So far Pamela's pride had kept her from marching up to Emerson's. But Hope, it appeared, had no intentions of coming home or calling. Should she send flowers, attempt a note, or simply kidnap her wife, drag her off somewhere until she saw sense again? Pamela toyed with her possibilities and went off in search of the fax. Despite her private disasters, she still had work to do.

Pamela was gazing out the window waiting for the fax to do its magic tricks when she saw them. Hope and Emerson were in the park on a blanket, talking. Emerson stroked Hope's cheek, kissed her gently, lingering. Hope held her tightly.

The fax buzzed, but Pamela stood with her hand limply on the machine. The clerk looked at her, inquiring if she needed something else. She said no and gathered up her papers.

She slipped past them and went next door to the library. Pamela tried to avoid the windows, which all faced the park below, but she couldn't resist. She found herself watching them. What was she really going to do? Could she afford to wait and see if the infatuation played itself out? Should she bow out and try for good graces, leaving the door open, waiting for Hope to walk back into her life? The thought of all that emptiness frightened her.

How did I ever let her get this far away from me? A small voice in the back of her head said, You were so busy being full of yourself that you couldn't see anything else. You let someone precious slip away.

Pamela spent the rest of the day at the library, trying to find solace in work. When the library closed she went to the house and upstairs to bed, avoiding everyone. The pain of realization had crept in, and she felt too vulnerable to be seen or touched by anyone. Tomorrow she would go see Hope . . . and learn to say good-bye.

Hope was relaxing in the tub, reading, and listening to Strauss — three of her favorite pastimes.

She looked up to see Pamela standing in the doorway. Emerson had gone to Grover's Corner to meet Lauren. Hope felt an instant knot of anxiety form in her stomach.

"I tried to knock, but the music was too loud," Pamela said. Standing there looking at Hope brought back a rush of memories about coming home and finding her like that, sitting on the commode telling Hope about her day. How many times she could have taken her to bed, made love to her, but she hadn't because she'd already done that and she was tired and sore. How many times she'd wrapped the towel around Hope, who kissed her, thinking about making love, and Pamela gently letting her down, promising later.

And now here she was, sitting in someone else's bathtub, looking more beautiful than she remembered.

"I need to talk to you," Pamela said.

"We've said everything, haven't we?" Hope said, looking around for a towel. The closest one was too far away.

"Need a towel?"

"Yes, please."

Pamela opened it up for her.

"I've seen you naked before, remember?"

"I know," Hope said, getting up and feeling anxious and shy.

Pamela looked at her. Hope looked away. Pamela guided her chin back to face her.

"I still love you. I'll always love you. And god knows I'm going to miss you, but I've come to say good-bye," Pamela said, feeling hot tears on her cheeks.

"Shh," Hope said, pulling her near, all resolve evaporating. "I'm sorry, I'm so sorry."

"I can't believe I'm losing you," Pamela said, beginning to sob.

"It'll be better in the end. You'll find someone who will be all the things you want, someone who won't disappoint you, someone who will love you the way you want."

"I had that someone and I let her get away," Pamela said, walking away from Hope.

Hope dressed and watched Pamela as she looked out the window.

"I should have called and told you instead of letting you find out like this. I didn't mean to be cruel. I just think that we let things go too far, and then there didn't seem a way back. It wasn't fair to keep you in the dark. I'm sorry," Hope said, walking to Pamela and standing beside her.

"I can't imagine my life without you in it, but I'm going to have to," Pamela said, turning toward her.

Hope touched her cheek and their eyes lingered. It was easier to be angry.

"Let's go get your stuff, and I'll take you to the airport."

"My flight's not until tomorrow."

"That's okay. We'll stay in Albuquerque. We'll say good-bye . . . away from everyone. I owe you that much."

"Hope, you don't owe me anything," Pamela said, starting to cry.

"I didn't mean it like that. I know it's hard to believe, but I still love you. I guess I thought I didn't anymore, but seeing you here, now, hurts," Hope said, swallowing hard and feeling tears starting to build.

"Shh, let's go," Pamela said.

"Wait, I've got to leave a note," Hope said.

"Okay, I'll wait outside."

Hope scribbled something, knowing it would be inadequate, thinking, Please, Emerson, understand this. She knew she wouldn't. But hopefully, Hope could repair the damage when she got back.

"She's gone," Emerson said, flying into the café.

"Who's gone?" Rachel asked.

"Hope," Emerson said, sitting at the counter and instantly burying her head.

"Where'd she go?" Berlin asked.

Emerson threw the note on the counter.

Katherine, Berlin, and Rachel read it.

"So?" Rachel asked. "She's coming back."

"You think so?" Emerson said.

"Of course. Taking someone to the airport doesn't mean she's leaving you," Berlin said.

"Well, yeah," Emerson said, beginning to look a little more hopeful. She was still scared. Hope with Pamela made her nervous. Maybe Pamela would cart Hope off and Emerson would never see her again.

"She wants to be with you. She'll be back," Rachel said.

"I hate to burst everyone's bubble, but Pamela's flight isn't until tomorrow," Katherine said.

"Why'd they leave now?" Emerson asked.

Berlin looked over at her and took Emerson's hand. "To say good-bye. Pamela needs this. Neither you nor Hope can deprive her of it. But Emerson, you're going to have to be strong. Part of new love is acknowledging old love. Don't go flipping out on us. I mean it."

Emerson stood up, "Okay. I understand." She walked out of the café. They watched her go.

"What the fuck," Rachel said.

"Excuse me, young lady," Berlin said.

"I wonder who I learned it from."

"Berlin, that was queer. Is she going to be all right?" Katherine said.

"Yes, she's going to be fine. Emerson is growing up."

"How do you know that?" Rachel asked.

"Because she understands about saying good-bye. It takes a grown-up to do that. Maybe someday you will do the same, Rachel," Berlin said, giving her a gentle tap.

"Excuse me," Rachel said.

"But first she has to learn to say hello," Katherine chided.

"We're not talking about me here."

"Yes, we are. You're the one who can't let Hope or Emerson go. You still haven't said good-bye."

Rachel stared at them. "But I'm going to have to."

"Emerson will be all right. Hope is getting to do what Angel needed to do with Emerson but never had the courage. Running off really is the worst way to end a love affair. People have things they need to say to each other. And they need the chance to do it. Take that away, and they become obsessed because they're always having one-sided conversations; the perpetual argument goes unfinished. We like finality. We need it," Berlin said.

"I'll drive," Hope said, taking the keys from Pamela, who looked distressed.

Hope put her bags in the trunk, grabbed the Ferrari guide from the hall table, and told Pamela to look for a nice B and B in Albuquerque.

"You act like we're going on vacation," Pamela said.

"We can make this better than it is. Let's try, okay?"

"Okay," Pamela said, getting in the car.

Pamela watched as Hope drove them out of town and on to the freeway. She seemed so different now. More confident, more sure of herself than Pamela had ever seen her. Hope looked over at her and smiled. She took her hand and kissed it. Pamela smiled back, feeling tears again. This was the hardest thing she'd ever done.

"This is not going to be easy," Pamela said.

"I know. We don't have to stop knowing each other. It'll be hard for a while, but you are an important part of my life. If I don't have to leave off being friends with you, I won't. That's up to you."

"Hope . . ."

"You don't have to answer now. I don't expect to have my cake and eat it too."

"Hope, I love you. I will always love you."

"Will you promise me something?"

"Yes."

"When you find the right one, promise that you won't cheat, that you'll give all of yourself and not just pieces, and that you'll pay attention. There's no worse love, Pamela, than distracted love. Make someone a good wife."

"I'll try," Pamela said, feeling tears run down her face.

"Don't cry. You'll make me cry, and then I can't drive."

They found the bed-and-breakfast. It was a charming Victorian house, quite out of place in its desert surroundings, but it was quaint and quiet and much better than the sterility of the average hotel. Hope didn't want the last time they were together to be cold and nondescript. Good-bye should be more than that.

"Shall we have something brought up, or do you want to go out?" Hope asked.

"Stay in with several bottles of wine," Pamela said, sinking into the bed and closing her eyes. Today had been a very long day, she thought to herself. Tomorrow would be even worse.

Hope ordered dinner and two bottles of wine. She watched Pamela resting and wondered what she was thinking.

They ate quietly, letting the wine ease out the tension they were feeling. Hope kept thinking, How do you say good-bye? They began by telling each other remember-when stories. Somehow that helped, telling the past, laughing about it.

"I know I botched things, Hope, but I never stopped loving you. I want you to know that," Pamela said, as they perused the family photo album

Hope had grabbed at the last minute as they were leaving. She thought it might be important.

"I know."

"Why did you bring this?" Pamela said, pointing to the album.

"I thought we might need it. I brought it with me this summer because I wanted to think about us and about what we'd become. I also brought your books and read them, trying to figure out more about you."

"And what did you figure out?"

"That you were in love with the wrong person."

"Why?"

"Because you need someone smart."

"You're smart."

"No, I'm animalistic and you're analytical. Not to say we haven't had some interesting moments. But I'll always disappoint you."

"And I'll always put a damper on whatever it is that moves you. I know there are things that move you, Hope. I know there are things you think about. You're different. I never took the time to figure out where or what you were up to, and I regret that now. Unfortunately, I can't fix it," Pamela said, turning the next page of the photo album.

"What do you think moves me?" Hope said, looking coyly at Pamela.

Pamela stroked Hope's face. "I can think of a few things."

"Such as?"

"Hope, if I didn't know better, I'd think you were propositioning me."

"I would never."

"You wouldn't? And why not?"

"I loved you most when you made love to me, because I knew then that you were mine, that all our differences melded."

"That won't work now, though, will it?" Pamela said, looking away, feeling sadness creeping up on her.

Hope kissed her long and hard. "I want to say good-bye."

"And this is how you want to do it?"

"Yes."

"Are you sure?"

"Very," Hope said, rolling Pamela on her back and straddling her stomach. Hope eased down on her. Pamela quivered beneath this familiar presence.

"Hope, I don't know."

Hope kissed away her protests, and Pamela let herself be seduced. Hope took off her shirt and Pamela suckled her breast, remembering the loving, and trying to savor each moment because it would be the last. It would have been so easy to get caught up in the lovemaking and to forget that this was the last time she would hold Hope, the last time she would take her in her mouth, the last time she would feel her long, smooth fingers inside her, and the last time she would cry out and still be hungry for more.

Pamela did all those things, remembering, forgetting, making love again and again, just like those wonderful first days of being in love, wishing they would never end, until finally exhausted they slept in each other's arms, dreading the morning.

When Hope got out of the shower, she found Pamela sitting on the edge of the bed, holding the photo album, and crying softly. She straightened up when she saw Hope.

"I'm sorry. I don't want to make it any harder than it is. I still can't believe that you're not coming back with me, that you will never be back," Pamela said, looking up at Hope.

Hope took Pamela's head and pressed it against her stomach, holding her there until she stopped crying.

"If we'd always been like this, you wouldn't be leaving," Pamela said.

Hope stroked her cheek. "I love you, and letting go is one of the hardest things I've ever done. But in the end it will save us both. It's hard to think that now."

"It's impossible."

"Pamela, you're strong. You'll get through this, and you'll be glad of it later."

"You sound like a therapist."

"No, I sound like Berlin."

"I liked Berlin, once I stopped being an asshole long enough to appreciate a few things. You never know. Maybe Emerson and I will be on speaking terms one day."

"You'd like her. She's just as staunch and pig-headed as you are."

"I am not," Pamela said, tackling Hope to the bed. She held her.

"Can I call you sometimes?" Pamela asked, looking more vulnerable than Hope had ever seen her.

"Yes. Now c'mon, we'd better get going."

"Call a cab, Hope. I'd rather leave you here than at the airport. It's too sad."

"Okay."

With tears running down her face and her hand pressed against the taxicab window, Hope let Pamela go, thinking, Please don't let this be the last time I see you.

Hope was beginning to understand how difficult it must have been for Emerson to let go of Angel, having not said good-bye and knowing she'd never see her again. It was strange. Three days ago she was furious with Pamela, and now she was sad and frightened.

Hope dashed upstairs, grabbed her stuff, paid the bill, and pulled away from the city, needing the drive in front of her.

She was halfway to Heroy when she pulled over at the wayside rest. The enormity of what she was doing hit her suddenly: This was truly the end. They had said good-bye, and there was no going back. She kept seeing Pamela's face through the cab window.

Hope sat on a rock that overlooked the valley and sobbed. She felt bad. Maybe it wasn't such a good thing saying good-bye this way. If only she hadn't seen the pain in Pamela's face. If she hadn't held her, made love to her that last time, maybe it would be easier. Those images are going to haunt me until the end of my days, Hope thought.

Would either Emerson or Hope ever be free of their past, or was Berlin right? You can love your girlfriend, but you must learn to live with her past because that will also be part of your relationship. Loving her is the easy part; dealing with the ghosts proves harder. Hope knew one thing for certain — she never wanted to hurt anyone else like she hurt Pamela. She too must make a better wife this time around.

Sixteen

"You look like perfect shit," Emerson said, smiling ear to ear and barely suppressing the urge to scoop Hope up in her arms and squeeze her hard. She looked fragile and tired.

"Well, there's a welcome home for you," Hope said, plopping down on the bed. She felt like she hadn't slept in weeks.

"Are you home?"

"Yes."

"I missed you. Are you all right?"

"I'm tired, and I'm kind of sad."

"It's hard to say good-bye."

"How are you doing?" Hope asked, thinking she'd been profusely in love with two women in the past couple of days and they had both taken a lot out of her.

"I thought about it, and I know you slept with her," Emerson said, sitting next to her.

Hope hung her head in utter resignation. "Great."

"You slept with her, right?"

"Yes, I slept with her."

"Okay, we've got that out of the way. What would you like for lunch? I'm famished."

"How can you eat at time like this?"

"It's easy. C'mon."

"Emerson, I can't go to lunch after I've confessed to adultery or whatever it is."

"I didn't mean to upset you. I wanted to know if you slept with her, that's all. You did. You didn't lie, so we move on."

"Just like that?"

"Yep. Now I know you don't lie. I trust you completely."

"Emerson . . ."

"Hope, I love you, and I understand. C'mon. Let's go eat, and then you can have a nap."

"You're back!" Rachel said, as they entered the café.

Hope sat down, looking the picture of dejection.

"What's wrong?" Rachel asked.

"She slept with Pamela," Emerson answered. "Do you have that tuna salad sandwich today?"

"What!" Rachel said, stopping in her tracks.

"The tuna salad sandwich," Emerson said.

"No, not that, the sleeping-with-Pamela part."

"Oh that. I don't know. Ask Hope."

Hope put her head down on the counter and groaned.

"What's wrong with Hope?" Berlin said, coming out of the kitchen.

"She slept with Pamela," Rachel replied.

"Saying good-bye, eh?" Berlin said, touching the top of Hope's head.

Hope looked up. "I can't believe we're having this discussion."

"Why not?" Emerson asked.

"Because it's not normal. I'm in love with you. I slept with my wife, and now I'm discussing it with my friends," Hope replied, looking completely puzzled.

"Ex-wife," Emerson corrected.

"Ex-wife."

"Is that what you want her to be?" Emerson asked.

"Yes, that's what she is."

"Good. Now about that sandwich."

"Emerson, I don't understand any of this," Hope said.

"What is there to understand? It's done."

"Aren't you mad?" Hope asked.

"Should I be?"

"I might be if it had been you," Hope replied.

"Yeah, but I slept with you when you were her wife, and you slept with her when you were my wife. Now Pamela and I are even."

"But what am I? A double adulteress."

"No, you're Hope and I love you," Emerson said, hugging her.

"Am I your wife?"

"I'd like you to be," Emerson said.

"Isn't that sweet," Berlin said.

"This is psychotic," Rachel said.

"Have a heart, Rachel," Berlin said.

"I do. I don't think I could let this fly, that's all."

"That's because you're an idealist who thinks everything is black and white, and it's not. God, how did you turn out to be so staunch," Berlin said.

"You know, I'm beginning to think that you don't like me as a daughter. You were always the one who defended me, and now all you do is criticize. Maybe you should find someone else to be your daughter since I don't seem to be what you want," Rachel said, storming out of the café.

"Oh this is just great!" Hope said, getting up and leaving.

Emerson and Berlin watched them go.

"Still want that tuna salad sandwich?" Berlin asked.

"Yeah."

"How come you're not running after them?"

"Because what's bothering them doesn't really have anything to do with me. They both need to chill. I'll eat. Hope will have a nap, and later we can all talk about it."

"Emerson, I want you to know that I'm really proud of you. You're growing up, and you're doing it very well."

"Thanks. Now where's my sandwich? I'm starving."

"Does love give you an appetite?"

"Yes."

"Good."

"Rachel, wait," Hope said, coming up behind her. Rachel turned. "What are you doing?"

"I don't know. I'm confused."

"Do you still love Pamela?"

"In a way. But I want to be with Emerson."

"So why did you sleep with her?"

"I don't know really. We were there, talking and remembering, and then it just happened. I don't regret it."

"Hope, how can you say that? You've committed a major indiscretion here. Starting life with Emerson on the coattails of this disaster, and that's all right."

"We started things long before that. Why are you so upset about this?"

"I don't know. I just am."

"Let's go have a drink and talk. I feel the need for a stiff scotch."

"All right. You look awful, you know. I suppose you were up most of the night fucking."

"Rachel, let it be."

"I can't."

"Can you at least wait until we get to the bar?"

"All right."

* * * * *

The saloon was quiet. They took a table in the back. Hope sipped her scotch slowly while Rachel downed two shots of tequila with a beer chaser.

"I don't know how you do that."

"Do what?" Rachel asked.

"Tequila with a beer chaser."

"I never could understand how you drink that shit."

"Scotch is good."

"An acquired taste, I guess."

"Rachel, what's really wrong?"

"I'm not the one who has any explaining to do."

"But you do. You're the only one who is upset by it."

"I just don't think that sleeping with Pamela was a good idea. It's not proper closure, and I think in the end it will hurt all of you."

"Why?"

"Because you're sending mixed signals. You tell Pamela good-bye but you make love, then you come back and tell Emerson. What is she supposed to think? Maybe you are done with Pamela and maybe you aren't. That's not good."

"You're never done with people, Rachel. Your relationship with them may change, but all the people who come through your life stay with a part of it. It's not like a term paper that you turn in and then it's over."

"I know."

"Do you though?"

"I don't know. I really need to let go of some

things, and I'm having a hard time doing it. Berlin's right. I need to learn to say good-bye. But I just can't seem to let go."

"Of Emerson?"

"Emerson and . . . you. I love you, Hope. I always have. I never thought Pamela would let you go. The pains of an unrequited love. So there you have it. I confess."

"Rachel —"

"Don't say it. I know. You never thought about me that way. No one ever does."

"Lily does. Only you won't let her inside. You hide things from her. Pamela used to do that to me. It's a bad thing, Rachel. You've got to learn to share yourself."

"You sound like Berlin."

"Maybe I'll grow up to be just like her," Hope said, leaning back in the booth.

Rachel ordered another round.

"Now tell me what you're going to do this semester?"

"Same old shit. Hide out from your ex-wife. Lily might transfer. She's close anyway. I don't want her to do anything she might regret."

"You've got to take some chances. A safe life is a sterile life. Sometimes messy is best."

"What are you going to do?"

"I get my trust in December, and I am toying with the idea of a bookstore. That's my latest scheme."

"What about the chickens?"

"I can have chickens and a bookstore. I want to

have a home. A real home, dinner at six, a garden, cocktails on the porch with a swing, chickens and little creatures everywhere."

"I never would have taken you for a country gal."

"The city made me thin, nervous, and pale. I like it here."

"I'm glad."

"Are you?"

"Yes, now drink up. I'm sure your wife is eagerly awaiting your arrival."

"Which wife?"

"You're teasing, I hope."

"I am."

Emerson wasn't home when Hope got there. Hope lay on the bed to wait and promptly fell asleep.

That's how Emerson found her, one lithe arm hanging off the edge of the bed, a mess of blond hair against the pillow. She grabbed her sketch pad and slowly drew, each line a tribute to love.

She couldn't believe that this lovely woman lying in her bed wanted to be her wife, that Hope had left another woman because she was madly in love with Emerson.

Maybe the Goddess had put her through hell so she'd find Hope and they'd make a life together. All she wanted was to come home each night and be with Hope, have a house together, wake up next to her, and buy a bed and a table and all those little domestic things that Emerson had shunned, thinking them mundane. Now she craved them. I want to sit across the dinner table from you and know that later I'll hold you in my arms, this night and every night.

Hope stirred and opened her eyes to find Emerson watching her.

"I wasn't drooling, was I?"

"No. I'm sorry. I know it's rude to watch someone sleep. People are so vulnerable then, but I couldn't help myself."

"Come here, my little voyeur."

Emerson took her in her arms.

"You're really staying here with me," Emerson asked.

"Of course, silly. Loose ends all tied up into a neat little knot . . ."

"Of broken hearts," Emerson said.

"You feel for her, don't you?"

"I can't imagine my life without you in it. Losing hurts."

"You're so sensitive, and that's why I love you."

"Is she going to be all right?"

"I don't know. I hope so. You didn't do anything, Emerson, except fall in love with someone who loved you back. Please don't feel bad."

"But you feel bad."

"I do, but I can't stay with her because I feel bad."

"I know, and I don't want you to. I may be sensitive, but I'm also greedy. I want you all to myself."

"Now about that sandwich."

"You're hungry?"

"Yes."

"Me too," Emerson said, kissing Hope's neck and reaching for her breast.

"But not for food?" Hope said, running her fingers through Emerson's hair as her lover's lips made a trail down her stomach.

"No, not for food."

"I guess the sandwich can wait," Hope said, closing her eyes.

A few of the publications of
THE NAIAD PRESS, INC.
P.O. Box 10543   Tallahassee, Florida 32302
Phone (850) 539-5965
Toll-Free Order Number: 1-800-533-1973
Mail orders welcome. Please include 15% postage.
Write or call for our free catalog which also features an
incredible selection of lesbian videos.

POSSESSIONS by Kaye Davis. 240 pp. 2nd Maris Middleton
Mystery.   ISBN 1-56280-192-9 $11.95

A QUESTION OF LOVE by Saxon Bennett. 208 pp. Every
woman is granted one great love.   ISBN 1-56280-205-4   11.95

RHYTHM TIDE by Frankie J. Jones. 160 pp. . . . to desire
passionately and be passionately desired.   ISBN 1-56280-189-9   11.95

PENN VALLEY PHOENIX by Janet McClellan. 208 pp. 2nd
Tru North Mystery.   ISBN 1-56280-200-3   11.95

BY RESERVATION ONLY by Jackie Calhoun. 240 pp. A
chance for true happiness.   ISBN 1-56280-191-0   11.95

OLD BLACK MAGIC by Jaye Maiman. 272 pp. 9th Robin
Miller Mystery.   ISBN 1-56280-175-9   11.95

LEGACY OF LOVE by Marianne K. Martin. 240 pp. Women
will do anything for her . . .   ISBN 1-56280-184-8   11.95

LETTING GO by Ann O'Leary. 160 pp. Laura, at 39, in love
with 23-year-old Kate.   ISBN 1-56280-183-X   11.95

LADY BE GOOD edited by Barbara Grier and Christine Cassidy.
288 pp. Erotic stories by Naiad Press authors.   ISBN 1-56280-180-5   14.95

CHAIN LETTER by Claire McNab. 288 pp. 9th Carol Ashton
mystery.   ISBN 1-56280-181-3   11.95

NIGHT VISION by Laura Adams. 256 pp. Erotic fantasy romance
by "famous" author.   ISBN 1-56280-182-1   11.95

SEA TO SHINING SEA by Lisa Shapiro. 256 pp. Unable to resist
the raging passion . . .   ISBN 1-56280-177-5   11.95

THIRD DEGREE by Kate Calloway. 224 pp. 3rd Cassidy James
mystery.   ISBN 1-56280-185-6   11.95

WHEN THE DANCING STOPS by Therese Szymanski. 272 pp.
1st Brett Higgins mystery.   ISBN 1-56280-186-4   11.95

PHASES OF THE MOON by Julia Watts. 192 pp. . . . . . hungry
for everything life has to offer.   ISBN 1-56280-176-7   11.95

LOVE OR MONEY by Jackie Calhoun. 240 pp. The romance of
real life.   ISBN 1-56280-147-3   10.95

SMOKE AND MIRRORS by Pat Welch. 224 pp. 5th Helen Black
Mystery.   ISBN 1-56280-143-0   10.95

DANCING IN THE DARK edited by Barbara Grier & Christine
Cassidy. 272 pp. Erotic love stories by Naiad Press authors.
                                               ISBN 1-56280-144-9   14.95

TIME AND TIME AGAIN by Catherine Ennis. 176 pp. Passionate
love affair.   ISBN 1-56280-145-7   10.95

PAXTON COURT by Diane Salvatore. 256 pp. Erotic and wickedly
funny contemporary tale about the business of learning to live
together.   ISBN 1-56280-114-7   10.95

INNER CIRCLE by Claire McNab. 208 pp. 8th Carol Ashton
Mystery.   ISBN 1-56280-135-X   11.95

LESBIAN SEX: AN ORAL HISTORY by Susan Johnson.
240 pp. Need we say more?   ISBN 1-56280-142-2   14.95

WILD THINGS by Karin Kallmaker. 240 pp. By the undisputed
mistress of lesbian romance.   ISBN 1-56280-139-2   11.95

THE GIRL NEXT DOOR by Mindy Kaplan. 208 pp. Just what
you'd expect.   ISBN 1-56280-140-6   11.95

NOW AND THEN by Penny Hayes. 240 pp. Romance on the
westward journey.   ISBN 1-56280-121-X   11.95

HEART ON FIRE by Diana Simmonds. 176 pp. The romantic and
erotic rival of *Curious Wine*.   ISBN 1-56280-152-X   11.95

DEATH AT LAVENDER BAY by Lauren Wright Douglas. 208 pp.
1st Allison O'Neil Mystery.   ISBN 1-56280-085-X   11.95

YES I SAID YES I WILL by Judith McDaniel. 272 pp. Hot
romance by famous author.   ISBN 1-56280-138-4   11.95

FORBIDDEN FIRES by Margaret C. Anderson. Edited by Mathilda
Hills. 176 pp. Famous author's "unpublished" Lesbian romance.
                                               ISBN 1-56280-123-6   21.95

SIDE TRACKS by Teresa Stores. 160 pp. Gender-bending
Lesbians on the road.   ISBN 1-56280-122-8   10.95

HOODED MURDER by Annette Van Dyke. 176 pp. 1st Jessie
Batelle Mystery.   ISBN 1-56280-134-1   10.95

WILDWOOD FLOWERS by Julia Watts. 208 pp. Hilarious and
heart-warming tale of true love.   ISBN 1-56280-127-9   10.95

NEVER SAY NEVER by Linda Hill. 224 pp. Rule #1: Never get
involved with . . .   ISBN 1-56280-126-0   11.95

THE SEARCH by Melanie McAllester. 240 pp. Exciting top cop
Tenny Mendoza case.   ISBN 1-56280-150-3   10.95

FOR LOVE AND FOR LIFE: INTIMATE PORTRAITS OF
LESBIAN COUPLES by Susan Johnson. 224 pp.

ISBN 1-56280-091-4   14.95

DEVOTION by Mindy Kaplan. 192 pp. See the movie — read
the book!   ISBN 1-56280-093-0   10.95

SOMEONE TO WATCH by Jaye Maiman. 272 pp. 4th Robin
Miller Mystery.   ISBN 1-56280-095-7   10.95

GREENER THAN GRASS by Jennifer Fulton. 208 pp. A young
woman — a stranger in her bed.   ISBN 1-56280-092-2   10.95

TRAVELS WITH DIANA HUNTER by Regine Sands. Erotic
lesbian romp. Audio Book (2 cassettes)   ISBN 1-56280-107-4   16.95

CABIN FEVER by Carol Schmidt. 256 pp. Sizzling suspense
and passion.   ISBN 1-56280-089-1   10.95

THERE WILL BE NO GOODBYES by Laura DeHart Young. 192
pp. Romantic love, strength, and friendship.   ISBN 1-56280-103-1   10.95

FAULTLINE by Sheila Ortiz Taylor. 144 pp. Joyous comic
lesbian novel.   ISBN 1-56280-108-2   9.95

OPEN HOUSE by Pat Welch. 176 pp. 4th Helen Black Mystery.

ISBN 1-56280-102-3   10.95

ONCE MORE WITH FEELING by Peggy J. Herring. 240 pp.
Lighthearted, loving romantic adventure.   ISBN 1-56280-089-2   11.95

FOREVER by Evelyn Kennedy. 224 pp. Passionate romance — love
overcoming all obstacles.   ISBN 1-56280-094-9   10.95

WHISPERS by Kris Bruyer. 176 pp. Romantic ghost story.

ISBN 1-56280-082-5   10.95

NIGHT SONGS by Penny Mickelbury. 224 pp. 2nd Gianna
Maglione Mystery.   ISBN 1-56280-097-3   10.95

GETTING TO THE POINT by Teresa Stores. 256 pp. Classic
southern Lesbian novel.   ISBN 1-56280-100-7   10.95

PAINTED MOON by Karin Kallmaker. 224 pp. Delicious
Kallmaker romance.   ISBN 1-56280-075-2   11.95

THE MYSTERIOUS NAIAD edited by Katherine V. Forrest &
Barbara Grier. 320 pp. Love stories by Naiad Press authors.

ISBN 1-56280-074-4   14.95

DAUGHTERS OF A CORAL DAWN by Katherine V. Forrest.
240 pp. Tenth Anniversay Edition.   ISBN 1-56280-104-X   11.95

BODY GUARD by Claire McNab. 208 pp. 6th Carol Ashton
Mystery.   ISBN 1-56280-073-6   11.95

CACTUS LOVE by Lee Lynch. 192 pp. Stories by the beloved
storyteller.   ISBN 1-56280-071-X   9.95

SECOND GUESS by Rose Beecham. 216 pp. An Amanda
Valentine Mystery.   ISBN 1-56280-069-8   9.95

A RAGE OF MAIDENS by Lauren Wright Douglas. 240 pp.
6th Caitlin Reece Mystery. ISBN 1-56280-068-X 10.95

TRIPLE EXPOSURE by Jackie Calhoun. 224 pp. Romantic
drama involving many characters. ISBN 1-56280-067-1 10.95

PERSONAL ADS by Robbi Sommers. 176 pp. Sizzling short
stories. ISBN 1-56280-059-0 11.95

CROSSWORDS by Penny Sumner. 256 pp. 2nd Victoria Cross
Mystery. ISBN 1-56280-064-7 9.95

SWEET CHERRY WINE by Carol Schmidt. 224 pp. A novel of
suspense. ISBN 1-56280-063-9 9.95

CERTAIN SMILES by Dorothy Tell. 160 pp. Erotic short stories.
ISBN 1-56280-066-3 9.95

EDITED OUT by Lisa Haddock. 224 pp. 1st Carmen Ramirez
Mystery. ISBN 1-56280-077-9 9.95

WEDNESDAY NIGHTS by Camarin Grae. 288 pp. Sexy
adventure. ISBN 1-56280-060-4 10.95

SMOKEY O by Celia Cohen. 176 pp. Relationships on the
playing field. ISBN 1-56280-057-4 9.95

KATHLEEN O'DONALD by Penny Hayes. 256 pp. Rose and
Kathleen find each other and employment in 1909 NYC.
ISBN 1-56280-070-1 9.95

STAYING HOME by Elisabeth Nonas. 256 pp. Molly and Alix
want a baby . . . or do they? ISBN 1-56280-076-0 10.95

TRUE LOVE by Jennifer Fulton. 240 pp. Six lesbians searching
for love in all the "right" places. ISBN 1-56280-035-3 11.95

KEEPING SECRETS by Penny Mickelbury. 208 pp. 1st Gianna
Maglione Mystery. ISBN 1-56280-052-3 9.95

THE ROMANTIC NAIAD edited by Katherine V. Forrest &
Barbara Grier. 336 pp. Love stories by Naiad Press authors.
ISBN 1-56280-054-X 14.95

UNDER MY SKIN by Jaye Maiman. 336 pp. 3rd Robin Miller
Mystery. ISBN 1-56280-049-3. 11.95

CAR POOL by Karin Kallmaker. 272pp. Lesbians on wheels
and then some! ISBN 1-56280-048-5 10.95

NOT TELLING MOTHER: STORIES FROM A LIFE by Diane
Salvatore. 176 pp. Her 3rd novel. ISBN 1-56280-044-2 9.95

GOBLIN MARKET by Lauren Wright Douglas. 240pp. 5th Caitlin
Reece Mystery. ISBN 1-56280-047-7 10.95

FRIENDS AND LOVERS by Jackie Calhoun. 224 pp. Mid-
western Lesbian lives and loves. ISBN 1-56280-041-8 11.95

BEHIND CLOSED DOORS by Robbi Sommers. 192 pp. Hot,
erotic short stories. ISBN 1-56280-039-6 11.95

CLAIRE OF THE MOON by Nicole Conn. 192 pp. See the
movie — read the book!   ISBN 1-56280-038-8   10.95

SILENT HEART by Claire McNab. 192 pp. Exotic Lesbian
romance.   ISBN 1-56280-036-1   10.95

THE SPY IN QUESTION by Amanda Kyle Williams. 256 pp.
A Madison McGuire Mystery.   ISBN 1-56280-037-X   9.95

SAVING GRACE by Jennifer Fulton. 240 pp. Adventure and
romantic entanglement.   ISBN 1-56280-051-5   10.95

CURIOUS WINE by Katherine V. Forrest. 176 pp. Tenth Anniver-
sary Edition. The most popular contemporary Lesbian love story.
                                       ISBN 1-56280-053-1   11.95
        Audio Book (2 cassettes)   ISBN 1-56280-105-8   16.95

CHAUTAUQUA by Catherine Ennis. 192 pp. Exciting, romantic
adventure.   ISBN 1-56280-032-9   9.95

A PROPER BURIAL by Pat Welch. 192 pp. 3rd Helen Black
Mystery.   ISBN 1-56280-033-7   9.95

SILVERLAKE HEAT: A Novel of Suspense by Carol Schmidt.
240 pp. Rhonda is as hot as Laney's dreams.   ISBN 1-56280-031-0   9.95

LOVE, ZENA BETH by Diane Salvatore. 224 pp. The most talked
about lesbian novel of the nineties!   ISBN 1-56280-030-2   10.95

A DOORYARD FULL OF FLOWERS by Isabel Miller. 160 pp.
Stories incl. 2 sequels to *Patience and Sarah.*   ISBN 1-56280-029-9   9.95

MURDER BY TRADITION by Katherine V. Forrest. 288 pp. 4th
Kate Delafield Mystery.   ISBN 1-56280-002-7   11.95

THE EROTIC NAIAD edited by Katherine V. Forrest & Barbara
Grier. 224 pp. Love stories by Naiad Press authors.
                                       ISBN 1-56280-026-4   14.95

DEAD CERTAIN by Claire McNab. 224 pp. 5th Carol Ashton
Mystery.   ISBN 1-56280-027-2   9.95

CRAZY FOR LOVING by Jaye Maiman. 320 pp. 2nd Robin Miller
Mystery.   ISBN 1-56280-025-6   10.95

STONEHURST by Barbara Johnson. 176 pp. Passionate regency
romance.   ISBN 1-56280-024-8   9.95

UNCERTAIN COMPANIONS by Robbi Sommers. 204 pp.
Steamy, erotic novel.   ISBN 1-56280-017-5   11.95

These are just a few of the many Naiad Press titles — we are the oldest and
largest lesbian/feminist publishing company in the world. We also offer an
enormous selection of lesbian video products. Please request a complete
catalog. We offer personal service; we encourage and welcome direct mail
orders from individuals who have limited access to bookstores carrying our
publications.